The Chosen Child

by

Joan Hall

This is a work of fiction. The events and characters portrayed are products of the author's imagination. Any resemblance to real life situations or persons is purely coincidental.

Copyright © 2009 by Joan Hall
ALL RIGHTS RESERVED
No portion of this publication may be reproduced, stored in any electronic system or transmitted in any form or by any means without written permission from the author. Brief quotations may be used for literary reviews.

ISBN: 978-0-615-23329-1

Cover designed by Pauletta Cook

282 St. Hwy. 1662
Olive Hill, KY 41164

Dedication

This book is dedicated to the wonderful people of eastern Kentucky especially those who live in Carter County. They are kind folk with easy smiles and neighborly ways. I share with them a life of incredible beauty within Kentucky's sheltering hills. We also share a heritage, one I like to explore with my imagination. I'm always wondering *what if*.

Forward

Let's talk about faith. I am referring to the values, beliefs and morals that make one appreciate something much larger than oneself. The emotion is an underlying character in this thought-provoking work, <u>The Chosen Child</u>. Sixteen-year-old Abigail Potter embodies faith, making her a unique character in Kentucky literature. In this story, Abigail is forced to make a decision, igniting a chain of events that spiral through this novel like a sparrow in the wind. Her heart is led by faith through a great tale full of twists and turns that kept this reader flipping the pages until well after the midnight hour. The message of Abigail's faith is a testimony to the loyalty of family, the bounds of perseverance in the wake of loss, and the walk in which faith transform us all. Joan Hall has created a story that is heartfelt and moves across the page as swiftly as lightning. This Appalachian story is a period tale about the lengths we'll go to protect those we love. The story of Abigail in <u>The Chosen Child</u> is definitely chosen to be a story about the testament of one's faith and destined to be a great piece of Kentucky literature.

John Braxton Sparks
Author of Lost: A Haunting in Appalachia,
The Darkest Hours: A Collection, and Ledge

Chapter One

August 14, 1938

Carter County, Kentucky

I recalled the time I dreamed of my wedding night. My tall, handsome young groom lifted me in his arms and carried me over the threshold of our small cottage. "I love you," he whispered in my ear. I giggled in my happiness as I wrapped my arms around his neck and snuggled close.

"Come on, Abby, stop dawdling." The harsh words jarred me back to reality. Luke Johnson had climbed from the car and stood on the porch steps. Evening shadows gathered in the eaves and around his tall male form. His large stooped frame bore the burden of his sixty years. Twilight glanced over his face, brushed the angles of his nose and jaw with light and cast darkness about his eyes and sunken cheeks making him appear hollow, like an empty, soulless vessel. Papa said we were all God's vessels and we should fill them with good food, good deeds and clean thoughts. I shuddered. Luke gestured impatiently with his large hand for me to follow.

My fingers shook as I reached behind the car seat and grabbed the paper bag that held my other Sunday dress, sandals, undies and my everyday wear. I had packed the new plastic comb Papa purchased for me, but gave the matching brush to my sister, Lucy. A brush was the only way to tame her mane of burnished curls. I decided to leave my box of treasured books in the car and retrieve them later, except for my copy of Heidi. She was my heroine and would give me strength through the next hours if I kept her near. I needed strength; oh how I needed strength. My heart cried out in silent anguish. *I can't be married to old Luke Johnson. I'm only sixteen years old.*

"Abigail." Luke's voice grated loud and hard.

"Oh, Lordy," I cried. I knew I couldn't postpone the inevitable any longer and opened the vehicle door. With a deep breath of nervous resolve, I climbed from the car. Surely Luke wouldn't be as frightful as I had imagined. I mustn't give in to my childish fears. An aching lump swelled in my throat and I swallowed hard. My feet moved in baby steps toward him. I glanced up at the aged two-story structure that was to be my

The Chosen Child   *Joan Hall*

new home. The house sagged against the side of the hill as if in need of support. Yellow glowed dimly from shrouded windows upstairs. Out of the dusk, stone chimneys stretched skyward on either side of the once-white clapboard house, like tortured arms reaching toward heaven in an appeal for divine intervention. *Oh please intervene.*

I clutched my arms around myself to stop the trembling that seized my body. Quietly, meekly, I joined my husband. He pulled a white handkerchief from his pants pocket then wiped away beads of sweat that had formed on his flushed face. The mid-August heat lay like a heavy, smothering blanket, yet I shivered.

Luke pushed open the heavy wooden door; the hinges creaked. He reached inside to flick on the overhead electric light. The glare of the bare yellow bulb cast a harsh brightness upon the living room. "Come on in, Abby," he commanded. I did. A thick layer of dust covered the sparse furnishings scattered about the room. My hand flew to my mouth and a cough itched at my throat. The stale air seemed unmoved, and reminded me of the old chest stored in the attic at home. I had curiously lifted the lid one day but dropped it quickly and held my nose in distaste.

A sagging old green sofa squatted against one wall. Above it hung a faded print of a beautiful guardian angel with arms outstretched. She stood in a protective pose above two small children who were crossing a bridge that spanned a churning creek. *Where is my guardian angel?* Silently I lifted my eyes heavenward.

My gaze slid to mud caked boots piled in a corner, a mangled heap of worn heels and stubby toes. I sighed in distress. So dirty was the hand crocheted rug on the floor that the colors were barely discernible, but spots of red and green yarns gave subtle clues.

Worst of all, was the sight of a lanky brown and white spotted bitch dog lying on a big overstuffed chair, sprawled with filthy paws dangling over the sides. The hound lifted her bony head and gave me an appraising stare from large chocolate colored eyes. Evidently finding me to be of no interest, she snuggled back onto the cushion with her long ears fanning out on either side of her face.

"You can put your things in there." Luke lifted his hand and pointed the way to an adjoining room. Numbly I moved in the direction of his extended finger, but stepped carefully around the litter. After closing the door behind me, I inspected my new sleeping place. The papered walls were yellowed and smudged with soot. The trailing vine pattern encircled the room like an entangled prison of which I couldn't break free. Filmy cobwebs hung from the ceiling like wispy tentacles ready to

The Chosen Child   *Joan Hall*

grab me. The rose patterned covers on the big four-poster bed appeared none too clean either. A year had passed since Luke's wife, Chloe passed away and the house had evidently been untouched ever since. I drew a long breath to calm myself.

This place sure needs a woman's touch again. It will take me a month to get it back in order. I tucked my clothing (except my cotton nightgown) in a bureau drawer and lay my copy of Heidi on top within my view. A mumbling of male voices vibrated through the thin wall that separated the bedroom from the living room. I recognized Doyle and Edward's voices. Doyle, the eldest of Luke's two sons had a deep throaty sound like his dad's. Quietly, I tiptoed over to the wall to better hear the words they spoke.

"Well, you pulled it off, old man." Doyle said in a gloating voice. "You married little Abigail Potter! You're smarter than I thought you were. You got yourself a child bride, Pa." I could picture the snickering face of Luke's son.

Laughter born of animal instinct bellowed from Luke. "You can still learn a few things from your Pa, Doyle" His voice lifted with thick smugness. "I saw what I wanted and I went after it, and that was Abigail Potter - now my wife, Mrs. Luke Johnson."

"What'd you do, Pa? It had to be something mighty low-down. Ain't no way Ezra Potter would give up his young

The Chosen Child   *Joan Hall*

daughter like that" The sting of disdain tightened Edward's controlled young voice.

When I heard Edward's wrathful tone, I thought, *he's not like his father, more like his dear mother.*

Edward didn't receive an immediate answer, so, again, he asked, "What'd you do to make Ezra Potter agree to such a thing? He's a good man and loves Abigail too much to marry her off like that."

"He's stupid," Luke answered in a hardened tone, hushing his younger son. "You can just get off your high horse, boy. Don't you go looking down your young nose at me. I don't have to do no explaining. I'm still your Pa and what I say and do is the law in this house and it ain't to be questioned. Is that clear?"

"Yeah, Pa," Edward agreed in a resigned, almost dead manner.

"Break out the jug, Doyle; let's have a drink," Luke said. I heard the sloshing of liquor. "To my marriage, boys, may it be a long and enjoyable union." The clank of china followed.

"Now, if you boys'll excuse me, I got a little bride waiting for me. I aim to teach her the ways of the world."

An involuntary shudder rocked me at the tone of Luke's voice. His clumping footsteps advanced him toward the room where I cowered. Just as the door burst open, I managed to push away from the wall. My heart thumped so loudly I could hardly hear above its pounding and my breaths were short and desperate.

"Well, my little bride, are you ready to go to bed?" Luke's eyes raked crudely over me as he pushed his hands through his oily gray hair. "You can't blame a man for being anxious on his wedding night." He grinned, showing yellowed teeth. He stood with legs braced apart as he lifted his arms out of his navy suit coat then tossed it carelessly onto a cane-bottom chair.

"It's only ten o'clock, Luke." I stumbled as I took a step backward. When I bumped against the wall and could recede no farther, I said, my voice trembling, "I'm just not sleepy yet." I twisted the red ribbon tie that adorned the waist of my wedding dress around a forefinger and slowly edged my way toward the door. "I think I'll go outside for a little while, to get a breath of fresh air. It's awfully warm in here."

"Oh no, you don't get away that easily." Luke jumped between me and the portal. "I'll raise the windows and make a draft, that'll cool the room down." He caught hold of my shaking hand. "Don't be afraid, Abby. I ain't gonna hurt you." His voice lowered to a deceptively soft whisper. The bright light glittered in his pale eyes. I thought of a serpent, coiled, ready to strike its victim.

"Doyle and Edward are just in the next room," I whispered, pulling my hand free of his clutching grasp. "Can't we wait until they go to bed?" The thought of Luke's boys on the other side of the thin wall filled me with shame. They would be able to hear the slightest sound. My cheeks grew hot at the thought.

"Those younguns will probably be up till twelve or so. I'm just too old to keep those hours." Luke held out his arms and spoke in a coaxing manner as if he were speaking to a young colt. "Come here like a proper bride and let me hold you."

"No," I whimpered, feeling like the helpless child that I was. I wanted to be held, but not by Luke Johnson. I sniffed as tears ran down my face. I wanted my mother.

A yearning for the touch of my Mama's hands washed over me, a need to be pulled to her frail breast and hear her say, "There, there, you're Mama's precious child and I'll take care of you." Often she had said those very words to me. But Mama was the one who needed care now.

"Quit that snivelin'; you're a big girl now, a married woman so act like one." Luke strode across the room toward me, each heavy footstep making me cringe. "You're mine, Abby," he growled, dropping the softer tone he had used earlier.

The Chosen Child   *Joan Hall*

"Bought and paid for, at a mighty high price too, I might add, and I aim to get my money's worth." He grabbed me by the arm and jerked me against him. A musty odor clung to his clothes and his breath reeked of hard liquor.

"You've been drinking," I gasped, twisting my head away from him.

"It was just a toast - to my wedding night. A man has the right to celebrate such an occasion" He bent his head, bringing his mouth down on mine. His wet lips tasted of raw whiskey and tobacco. My stomach heaved and an odd buzzing sounded in my ears. I struggled uselessly against him as tears swelled again in my eyes.

"Let me go," I begged, in a low voice. Instead, Luke clutched me tighter.

He groaned. "I've finally got you, you're mine, forever, until death do us part." A deep guttural sound erupted from him and I almost fainted. He clutched my face tightly against his wrinkled shirt. I gasped for breath.

Terror clawed through me as I pushed uselessly against him. "You don't know how I've wanted you," he gasped in my ear. "I swear, you're the prettiest little thing I ever did see and now you're mine, all mine." His big hands jerked the pins from my hair, letting the locks sweep down my back. As I struggled, my hair swept round me like a cape. He wrapped his fingers in

The Chosen Child   *Joan Hall*

the mass and brought the strands up to his face and breathed deeply. "You're so fresh and new."

Luke shook like he was coming down with something. Maybe he was ill. I pulled my hand free and pressed my fingers against his forehead, desperate for an answer. He wasn't running a fever but there was sweat on his brow. "Are you sick?" I asked uneasily, my voice coming out weak and shaky. A man didn't act like this – like he wasn't right in his head. There had to be a reason.

Luke laughed, a low rumbling sound from deep within his chest. "I'm sick all right, sick from wanting you. I've got a fever but it ain't in my head, girl."

Realization hit me, bringing new fear. Now I understood. This was a man's passion and Luke was going to act on that emotion. When the ladies whispered about *the act* behind the palms of their hands, they giggled and spoke as if it were something to be enjoyed, but I found this meeting of bodies to be sickening. I wanted to retch but Luke held me too tightly. Suddenly he let me go and began stripping off his clothes. It was good to be free of his grasp if only for a short time, but I sensed there was worse to come. I turned my back to my husband as he flicked the light switch plunging the room into darkness.

It took a few seconds for my eyes to adjust to the loss of

The Chosen Child   *Joan Hall*

light but the moonbeam coming through the window enabled me to see. I lifted my arms and pulled my dress and petticoat over my head. Luke gasped like he drew his last breath. *If only he would fall over dead.* I cringed at the thought. How could I allow an idea like that to enter my head? Oh, I didn't wish such a thing to happen, but if it did, I wouldn't be greatly saddened. Luke drew a deep ragged breath and I knew he was still very much alive. What would happen now? Luke fell silent, like a stalking cat, waiting to pounce on his prey. My knees shook so badly I clutched the edge of the bureau for support. The stillness grew until I felt I would drown in it. My mind sought escape and began reliving the last days that had brought me to this end.

Chapter Two

Was it only a week ago that I sat on the varnished pew in our small church, an innocent child, unaware of the fate that was to befall me so soon? The vision of the interior of the church as it had been last Sunday evening soothed my troubled mind.

The day was sticky and blistering hot. All the windows were raised but not a breath of air entered, just a pesky fly that buzzed about my face. Sitting with my head bowed, I listened to the preacher's fervent prayer. Even with my eyes closed, I knew the scene around me. Preacher Allison knelt on his knees

The Chosen Child   *Joan Hall*

in the pulpit with a Bible gripped in one trembling hand and his other hand thrust toward Heaven. His voice thundered in rapture. Sweat poured from his wrinkled brow, coursed in rivulets over his round cheeks to mottle the starched collar of his white shirt.

"Oh, Heavenly Father," he pleaded. "Forgive us our sins and grant us mercy. Be with us always."

The elders were stooped with their knees on the rough plank floor. Their heads, cushioned by their folded arms, rested on the wooden pews. Through the murmuring crowd, their pleas trumpeted, "Bless us, Lord."

The creaky, old spring-wound paddle fan overhead barely stirred the hot still air of the summer evening. Around the walls black kerosene lanterns hung at intervals. The area around each was stained with soot. If someone turned the wicks too high, dark smoke swirled out of the glass chimneys. After years of use, the soot just could not be washed off. In the center of the building sat a pot-bellied stove. Atop it was a white enameled communal water bucket and dipper, ready to whet the thirst of any who needed a drink. The stove was lit only during winter months so in summer, could be put to other uses, like a table.

I whispered a dutiful, "Amen," and lifted my head. This was the time I enjoyed most, when I could observe my

The Chosen Child   *Joan Hall*

neighbors freely without their knowledge. My eyes sought Preacher Allison first. He knelt directly beneath the fan. The slight breeze lifted the sparse white hairs on his ancient head, making them spread out and flutter on either side like tiny gossamer angel wings. I smiled behind my cardboard fan. One day I would write stories like the ones I loved to read from my treasury of old books, like Emma, by Jane Austin. My favorite teacher, Mrs. Arnold, had passed on to me all the worn and ragged editions that were to be discarded from the school library. Carefully, I had taped and repaired each volume then stored them to bring out occasionally for an enjoyable read.

I would write about Preacher Allison I decided; he would be my hero. Heroes were not always young and beautiful. Well, mine wouldn't be. They would have round faces and rotund figures or work hardened hands and soft, brave hearts.

My eyes moved on to old Mr. McLean. His shiny bald head reflected the lamp light like a beacon when he rocked back and forth. Mischievously, I began to recite, "One if by day, two if by night." Restlessly, I moved on to my next subjects, Mr. and Mrs. Warden. She was round and lumpy like an over-stuffed feather pillow that needed plumping and he resembled a thin sapling with long branching arms and twig-like fingers.

I pulled a dainty embroidered handkerchief from the

The Chosen Child   *Joan Hall*

pocket of my cotton dress and dabbed at the beads of moisture gathered above my lip then wiped beneath my damp collar. I turned to better view the occupants across the aisle.

Luke Johnson's presence was inescapable, even in my thoughts, for he sat in his usual place in the second row of the church. He was a tall man with wide gaunt shoulders and stern-faced as always. I could find nothing amusing about him. His long brown hair, streaked with gray, was slicked back with too much oil and he had small squinty eyes. I had always thought of them as weasel eyes because they darted secretively. He had a long beak nose and when he blew it, made a loud honking noise, like a goose. A smile played at my lips. Luke's two sons accompanied him. Doyle resembled his dad in looks and temperament with the same tall figure and same scowling face.

Edward's face was unsmiling as well and his brow was furrowed. He had a quiet nature and stayed to himself a lot. About the only times I saw him was at the church meetings. Edward had taken it hard when his mother died. I could still recall the anguish in his eyes the day of her funeral. Luke was always too near him for me to say words of comfort.

Movement at my side drew my attention. Becky was getting restless. I pulled my baby sister onto my lap and hushed her as my eyes quickly swept the rest of my family. My three brothers, George, Josh and Paul, were sitting quietly for a

The Chosen Child   *Joan Hall*

change. They were usually a handful. Lucy, at thirteen, looked the demure young lady that she was.

A lump swelled in my throat when I gazed at my parents, Ezra and Molly. My mother's arms were pencil thin and her eyes had dark circles around them. Unnatural spots of reddish color dotted her thin cheeks. The urge to reach out and take her hand swelled inside me but her fingers were clasped by Papa. I stared at my handsome father. Deep creases plowed across his forehead, making him appear older than his forty years, but he was still a striking figure. He worked hard tending his fifty acre hillside farm. Many times I had heard him say how much he loved farming. "Farming is all I ever wanted to do," he had said and he was good at it. We were well fed from our big garden, fruit trees, chickens and cows. All we needed from the general store was flour, cornmeal, sugar and coffee for Papa. The tobacco crop paid for everything else we needed like clothes.

"Amen."

"Ah, thank you, Lord."

"Amen."

The prayer ended and heads were lifted, one after another, all over the church. Hands wiped handkerchiefs over reddened eyes and noses. Preacher Allison stood, a signal the meeting was concluded. I lifted Becky into my arms as Papa

The Chosen Child   *Joan Hall*

and Mama made their way up the aisle to shake the preacher's hand. I turned and hurried from the church, ushering the other children in front of me. Luke lounged against the outside of the building. Through the darkness, the light from the doorway glinted like shards of glass in his eyes.

"Evening, Abigail," he mouthed as I marched by.

The unsettling thought that he might grab me and pull me against his stooped body flashed through my mind. With compressed lips, I nodded my head to him in a mannerly fashion and rushed past. I lifted the children into the back of our wagon then climbed in myself. Becky settled onto my lap. My mother soon followed and climbed into the front seat. "Come on, Ezra," she called to my father, who was tarrying. Mama leaned forward in an uncomfortable pose and impatiently twisted the reins in her hands.

My gaze turned to the group standing about the churchyard as I searched for Papa. What was keeping him? I spied him standing next to Luke. Papa held his head low and twisted his hat in his hands. He scuffed a shoe back and forth in the dirt. I turned my head away, not understanding the uneasy bumps pricking my skin. I watched as Edward climbed into Luke's new black Chevrolet coupe. Luke had one of the four cars in the area. The other three belonged to the mortician, the man who owned the general store, and the Sheriff, who had an

The Chosen Child   *Joan Hall*

old station wagon. Everyone wondered how Luke could afford a car. His farm was larger than most other farms, it was true, but most of his fields lay untended. Papa had speculated that the money must have been inherited.

Finally, Papa climbed into the wagon beside Mama and took the reins. I drew a deep contented breath as I nuzzled the top of Becky's downy blond head. The baby's hair was almost as fair as my own. We were all a family of towheads except for Lucy, whose locks were the color of copper pennies. The wagon jostled noisily over the rutted path that led to our small clapboard house, but it didn't bother me. I loved riding the open wagon during the twilight hours. The hills loomed out of the dusk like a massive dark green fortress of hardwood trees and jagged rocky cliffs. A feeling of warmth and love enwrapped me like a blanket. The cabin soon came into view, nestled deep in a hollow tucked between two lofty hills. I felt our house snuggled against the bosom of the giant mother earth just over where her heart beat.

The locals say this is God's country, blessed abundantly by God himself as no other place. Some even refer to Kentucky as the *promised land* where all needs are fulfilled. Many times I had heard that phrase from Papa. He said, "There just ain't nowhere like these hills of eastern Kentucky." He should know for he spent four years in the navy, enlisting when he was

The Chosen Child   *Joan Hall*

eighteen years old. He saved his earnings and bought his farm when he got out.

"Abby, dear, will you put the children to bed? I'm awfully tired." My mother stood as if through great effort. Her skin appeared more pale than usual and her shoulders slumped forward. Her pretty pink dress hung on her slim shoulders. I would have to 'take it up' some more.

"Of course I will, Mama. You go on to bed and you can sleep late tomorrow, too. I'll get up and fix breakfast for Papa."

"You're a good and faithful daughter, Abby," Papa said as he put his arm around our mother and helped her toward their room. "I'll be needin' you bout five in the morning," he called over his shoulder.

"All right, Papa," I answered, glowing from his modest compliment. Within the hour the chore was completed and gratefully I blew out the light and climbed beneath the ragged patchwork quilt. With Becky snuggled close, I fell into serene sleep.

I found it difficult to climb out of bed before daylight but I dutifully threw back the covers, shivering when my warm feet touched the worn linoleum floor. After pulling my loose fitting dress over my head, I hurriedly combed my hair. I always let the locks fall loose around my shoulders while I slept, but it was much more practical by day to keep the mop

The Chosen Child   *Joan Hall*

twisted into a coil atop my head. My hair was much too curly, but when dampened, would stay restrained, except for a few stubborn wisps around my face. I checked my reflection in the ancient mirror. I had gotten many compliments on my hair. Papa called me corn silk when I was small because he said my hair reminded him of the pale creamy strands inside the husks of an ear of corn.

Peering at my reflection more closely, I touched a finger to my moist tongue, then in a futile effort, rubbed at the tiny smudges sprinkled across my nose. "I hate freckles." Mama had promised I would outgrow them, but there they were, for everyone to see. "Stubborn freckles," I moaned. "They're just like me, stubborn." I liked my eyes though. Two bright orbs of pale blue stared back at me. "They're the color of the sky, on a clear summer day." A smile revealed white straight teeth, a result of the cow's milk I drank as a child, I reckoned.

In a search for glowing embers, I stirred the ashes in the black iron cook stove. There were just enough to bring the kindling to a crackling warmth. While my father milked the cows, I made biscuits and gravy. He came inside just as I was taking the bread from the oven.

"Breakfast is ready, Papa. Sit down and eat while it's hot." He didn't reply but pulled out a chair and slumped into it. "What's the matter, Papa?" His worried frown bothered me.

The Chosen Child   *Joan Hall*

He lifted his gaze to me and sighed. "It's your Mama; she's not getting any better. Those vitamins the Doc gave her ain't helped at all and her cough is getting worse. I think I'd better take her over to that new clinic in Ashland."

"When are you leaving?" I asked as I placed a slice of hot cured ham on his plate. Wispy steam spiraled upward toward Papa's face, twisting and swaying like a fragrant temptress.

My father was not enticed, just stared at his plate. He stabbed at the pink slab of ham with his fork, pushing it from one side of his platter to the other. "Today," he answered, sighing heavily. "I'll hitch up the team as soon as it gets light enough. I don't look forward to that long trip and it'll be rough on Molly. You know she gets tired awful easy. You'll have to tend the children while we're gone. Make the boys pitch that hay I cut yesterday, and if there's time they can start topping the tobacco. We want the leaves to broaden out. Those plants don't need to get no taller. Maybe you and Lucy can start digging the potatoes and store them in the cellar."

"Yes, Papa, is there anything else?" Mentally I prepared for the long day's labor. I didn't mind, really. The sense of accomplishment I felt after a day in the fields was most gratifying and I usually had energy to spare.

"No, everything else can wait. We'll probably be gone

The Chosen Child   *Joan Hall*

all day. You know how those doctors' offices can be." His words sounded strained, like they were torn from him.

"Don't worry, Papa, I'll take care of everything while you're gone," I promised. Before he left the room he reached out and gently patted my cheek. He had never been a demonstrative man and a lump formed in my throat at the tender gesture. I loved my Papa and Mama so much there were no words to describe the depth of my feelings.

The sun climbed lazily over the hilltop. The big golden globe quickly chased away the dew and brought the sleepy hollow noisily to life. The rooster crowed raucously and strutted around the barnyard like a proud monarch. He ruffled his plumage in a regal manner and the chickens clucked contentedly in his shadow. The hogs gathered around the feed trough, squealing in greedy anticipation of the morning fare, a mass of round pink bodies and spiraling slim tails. The children were rising too, clamoring for their breakfast, their voices adding to the din of morning sounds. Lucy had taken over in the kitchen so I could care for the animals and help Papa prepare for the long ride. He hitched a pair of fresh prancing horses to the wagon. Morning light glistened over their russet colored coats. I arranged plump cushions on the hard wooden bench so Mama would be more comfortable, then placed a lunch basket in the back.

The Chosen Child   *Joan Hall*

"You shouldn't fuss over me so, daughter," my mother protested. "I'll get spoiled with all this attention." A brief bittersweet smile lighted her face for a moment when she gazed at me. Her small nose turned up slightly on the end and her skin was milky white. Lucy was the only child to inherit her ivory complexion. Mama was still beautiful despite her battle with ill health. She was just too delicate for the tedious life on a farm, and she had given birth too many times in too few years. I well remembered Becky's birth and how Mama suffered labor for days and recouped for weeks. I had struggled with the chore of caring for a sick mother and a newborn baby as well.

"You've been spoiling us for years," I responded. "It's about time it was returned. I've packed ham and biscuits and a jug of water for your lunch." Mama followed my pointing finger with her eyes. "Oh," I added. "There's a shawl too, in case it should turn cool. We sure don't want you catching cold or ...or anything like that." My voice faltered.

"Thank you, child." Mama smoothed her dress with a trembling hand then cleared her throat. "You're so thoughtful, Abby. You always were a very special child, always giving of yourself." She breathed a long sigh and tears rolled unheeded from her eyes. "Take good care of the children."

"Don't worry, Mama, I'll take care of everything while you're gone, I promise." Tears threatened in my own eyes.

The Chosen Child   *Joan Hall*

"You'll be fine, you'll see. There are good doctors in the city."
I knew my mother was getting weary of being sick all the time.
The new doctors in the city just had to make her better.

Papa climbed into the wagon beside his wife and teased
her. "I swear, Molly, you're the first woman I ever saw who
didn't want to be fussed over." She gave him an indulgent
smile and straightened her shoulders.

"Get up, Homer, Rufus, get up." Lifting the reigns, he
urged the horses forward. Mama sat stiffly beside him, staring
straight ahead. Just once she turned to look toward me and the
house. I called after them, "Be careful. Have a good trip," then
waved until they were out of sight.

Chapter Three

"When are Mama and Papa gonna get home?" George's voice was forlorn. He stood with the palms of his hands and his forehead pressed against the window pane. He appeared thin and waif-like in his oversized dungarees. The seat hung loosely behind and the legs were rolled up at the ankles. George, as the oldest boy received store-bought clothes. Mama always purchased his clothes a size larger than he needed. To get longer wear they were handed down to the other boys. Glancing at the clock, in surprise I found it was almost seven o'clock. Fear clawed at my stomach. They should have been back by now.

The Chosen Child   *Joan Hall*

"You kids go outside and play while it's still light." My voice squeaked, unnaturally tight and cross.

"There's nothing to play, besides I'm tired." Lucy complained, her bottom lip stuck out. She was spoiled. Often I would perform my own chores as well as hers just to avoid the nuisance of her complaining. The anxious, restless mood George displayed seemed to be spreading.

"You can always find something to do," I insisted. "Go wading in the creek. That will cool you off and make you feel better."

"I don't want to go wading," Paul, the youngest of the boys joined in. At six, he usually went the way of the majority.

"Well, go play ivy-over," I said, losing patience. "I'll make you a ball." I went in search of an old sock and found one beyond repair. After filling it with old rags, I tied it up with string and cut off the top. "Here," I said as I tossed it into the air toward George. "Now, go outside," I ordered. Something always needed mending, so I busied myself at the sewing machine. I had to stay occupied, keep my mind settled, and ward off the worry that haunted me. The children acted on my suggestion. I smiled at the boys' spirited call of "Ivy-over," as they tossed the ball over the top of the house, and the squeal of laughter when it was caught on the other side by Lucy. A playful game of tag ensued when Lucy tried to strike the boys

The Chosen Child   *Joan Hall*

with her catch. Becoming lost in my work, I didn't look up until I heard the children shouting.

"Here comes Papa."

"Papa is coming."

"Thank goodness," I sighed, a heaviness lifting from my heart. I wouldn't admit to myself how worried I had been. I dropped my sewing and rushed out onto the porch to meet them. A feeling of dread consumed me, stopping me short. Papa was climbing from the wagon and he was alone.

A chorus of childish voices greeted him, "Where's Mama?"

A redness rimmed Papa's eyes and his features sagged making him appear years older. His gaze swept from one child to another until he had encompassed all of us before he spoke. "I had to leave her at the clinic," he choked. "She has to stay there for awhile. When they have an opening at the sanitarium in Louisville, she'll be moved there."

"What's wrong with her, Papa?" I asked, although afraid to hear the answer.

"Consumption." his brief reply seemed wrenched from deep within him. He clutched the porch banister as if he hadn't the strength to bear the heavy burden resting on his narrow shoulders. He staggered beneath the weight.

"Oh no." I moaned. Without conscious thought, my

The Chosen Child   *Joan Hall*

hand flew to my throat where a pulse throbbed wildly. Our family was about to suffer a terrible trial.

"Poor Mama," Lucy cried, rushing over to our father and throwing her arms around his waist, burrowed her head against his chest.

Papa laid a hand on her head as his tortured eyes beseeched me, "T B is contagious; you kids are all at risk. The doctors have a skin test and they want me to bring you all in to the clinic as soon as possible so you can be checked."

My heart plummeted. As bad as the news was about Mama, the thought of one or more of the children being struck as well was more than a heart could tolerate. It just couldn't happen.

"I don't want no test," Josh cried out. "There's nothing wrong with me." I recognized the fear in his young face and hurried to reassure him.

"Josh, I know about the test. It's simply a scratch on your arm and doesn't really hurt, especially a tough guy like you." My words shushed the youngster, in fact he puffed out his chest at my compliment. I wished I could as easily calm my own fears. An apprehension settled somewhere inside me and caused my stomach to tighten. I knew I would not feel better until I was certain the rest of our family was healthy.

"After we go to the clinic, will we get to visit with

The Chosen Child   *Joan Hall*

Mama?" Lucy held a hopeful lilt to her voice. "I miss her already."

"Yes," Papa replied, trying his best to smile. "You'll get to see your mother." A chorus of gleeful shouts erupted but our father hushed them. "The visit will have to be brief. Your Mama needs her rest."

"Come on, Papa, I've got your supper in the warmer." My voice was strong and sure in spite of my quaking insides. Someone had to keep the family going I told myself.

Papa trudged silently into the house behind me, the children following closely behind him. We were all subdued for we had heard the dreaded word many times before and knew how grave the disease was that had struck our beloved mother. Becky seemed to sense the mood and stuck her fingers in her mouth while clutching at my skirt in a plea for comfort. I picked up the child and gave her a fierce hug.

After falling listlessly into a chair, our father dropped his head into his hands and moaned. "She should've had better care. Why didn't Doc Jones realize that Molly didn't have colds all this time?" He slapped his forehead with the palm of his hand. "I should've seen this coming. I'm with her every day. It's all my fault that she got so sick."

"Don't blame yourself, Papa; you know Mama has always been puny." I patted his shoulder in an attempt to give

The Chosen Child   *Joan Hall*

him comfort. "How could you know when something got seriously wrong with her health? She has always coughed, like when she got near the animals or strolled through the fields. How could we know her cough had changed?" I was feeling pangs of guilt too, for I had read articles in books about tuberculosis. There were definite signs of the disease and I hadn't recognized them.

"Lord have mercy; what am I gonna do without her?" A silent sob racked Papa's body. He wiped his hand across his eyes in an attempt to regain control.

"We'll get by somehow." I spoke in a soothing voice, rubbing my hands over his trembling shoulders. "You're awfully tired from the trip. Tomorrow things will look brighter. We'll take the children for their tests and visit Mama then the next night we'll go to church and request prayer for her. With the revival going on, everyone will be there. She'll be well again, you'll see."

"Thank you, Abby," Papa said, brightening a bit. "That's a good idea. We'll all pray for Molly's recovery." I could find no comfort for myself though my words sounded good even to my own ears. A coldness had settled in my chest making my heart constrict and pump harder, until its beat was all I could hear.

I wasn't looking forward to the long trek into Ashland.

The Chosen Child   *Joan Hall*

Mentally I plotted the day - on the road by six, clinic by ten, testing hopefully completed by twelve, a quick lunch in the wagon, on to the hospital for an hour with Mama and back home by six. We would all be exhausted even if everything went timely and no unforeseen problems arose.

The next morning, Josh rubbed sleep from his eyes as I herded him and the other kids out the door promptly at six o'clock. Thankfully, we had a clear sky, so the trip should be a pleasant one, weather wise. Papa had the wagon readied for the trip. The children piled in the back on the pallet I had made then I climbed on the seat beside him. There should be a couple hours peace for the kids would surely sleep another two hours. I spread a blanket over the mass of arms and legs. Quietness hung in the air. The only sound was the clopping horses' hooves against the packed dirt road. The birds hadn't even started their morning song.

"It's going to be another warm one," Papa said in a lowered tone mindful of the children asleep behind us. "At least we won't be traveling in the heat of the day." He drew a deep breath, inhaling the fresh scent of cut grasses that laced the air from a neighbor's hay stacks. "This is God's country, daughter, and we're God's people. He's going to take care of us." Papa's face took on a glow and he spoke in a reverent tone. "We just have to keep the faith and do his will."

The Chosen Child   *Joan Hall*

"Yes, Papa," I smiled. I had never questioned my faith. Belief had always been a vital part of my life, as certain as eating and sleeping. I conversed with God as easily as I talked to Papa. Although God had never answered me personally, he often spoke in deeds.

We passed several early travelers. Their faces were unfamiliar since we were traveling in the opposite direction that we normally took to Vanceburg. Two were on horseback, one in a wagon similar to our own and three were in vehicles, but they all spoke in friendly greeting.

About an hour and half into the ride, the children roused to full wakefulness. They sat quietly but listlessly at first. My heart went out to them all. "Papa, there's a creek over there where we can water the horses and maybe the kids can stretch their legs." Once we were stopped, I told the boys, "Go gather a pile of small stones and put them in the wagon."

"Why?" Paul demanded, needing a reason for everything.

"Because I said so," I returned in my firmest voice. After a short break and the boys had collected a neat pile of stones, we resumed out travel.

"What was that all about?" Papa inquired with a puzzled expression.

"You'll see," I replied in a teasing manner. Farther into

The Chosen Child   *Joan Hall*

the journey the restlessness began.

"George pulled my braid," Lucy cried out.

Then Josh complained, "Paul pushed me," and on it went.

"You kids behave back there," Papa yelled, to no avail.

I waited until the bantering became outright squabbles and Papa grew cross and threatened to pull over and cut a switch. It was time, I decided as I dug around in the bag at my feet, to retrieve the three slingshots I had made last evening and brought along.

"Wow, Abby," George exclaimed as I passed one to each boy.

"Now, make sure you aim only at trees or fence posts," I cautioned. Lucy gave me an expectant look as I brought out my half finished cross stitch sampler and threads and handed them to her. "Be careful with that needle," I warned. Finally for Becky, I lifted out her favorite baby doll, the one she loved to undress and dress.

"Ah, thank you, Abby," Papa sighed, noting the calming of the young ones' behavior. "You got anything in that bag for me?" he said, laughing. It was good to see my father smile. For a few minutes he was just as he used to be but I knew it couldn't last.

The sign at the junction read Route 60. "This paved

The Chosen Child   *Joan Hall*

road here will take us directly into Ashland," Papa said. "It'll only be a little ways now." As we neared the town, we saw few wagons. Cars of all shapes and sizes buzzed everywhere. Homer and Rufus grew agitated and Papa struggled to keep them under control. People turned to stare as we rolled by. I suppose we were a sight, with a wagon load of tassel haired kids. Papa kindly threw up his hand in greeting. "The hospital is at the end of this street," he said, his voice tightening in the now familiar way. He slapped the reigns against the horses' rumps, urging them down the paved road.

The red brick structure looked like a big rambling house, not quite what I had imagined. Standing two stories high, the building had a plain, undecorated exterior making it appear cold and uninviting. "First we go to the doctor's office for those tests then I'll take you to see your Mama."

"My, my, Mr. Potter, are all these kids yours?" The nurse made an attempt at friendliness with a smiling face as her eyes encompassed our family. For some reason I didn't take to her. "Well, let's get down to business," she said in a brusque manner. Pointing her finger in my direction where I held Becky on my lap, she said, "We'll start with the little one first."

Becky gazed up at me with puzzled eyes as I held her arm out toward the woman. "Now this will hurt just a little," the nurse said in a kinder voice as she dropped a spot of liquid

The Chosen Child   *Joan Hall*

on the baby's arm. As she busied herself, her eyes flicked over me. "My, my, aren't you a pretty one, and not a smidgen of makeup."

Her words made me note her appearance. Even though her complexion was of a darker tone than mine she appeared pale. Her lovely dark hair had been pulled back into a severe chignon and a black line had been drawn around her large amber colored eyes. She was very striking but not quite pretty. I guessed her age to be about thirty years. A wail of pain brought my attention back to the child on my lap.

"There, there, it's over," the nurse soothed, releasing Becky's arm. "Now it's your turn," she said, flicking her eyes over me.

Clutching the crying baby in one arm I stuck out my other arm. I closed my eyes and winced as a pain tore at my skin. In a flash it was done. "Next," she called out, dismissing us without another word. I had a sneaking suspicion my skin test had hurt more than it should have.

Moments later Papa and the boys received their tests. "I bet those sandwiches in the wagon would taste mighty good about now," I said in an attempt to draw their attention away from the smarting blemishes. Gleeful shouts from my brothers agreed. At the farthest end of the parking lot, we found a shady spot beneath a tall elm that was good for the horses. Like

The Chosen Child   *Joan Hall*

puppies, the boys jumped to the ground and rolled around on the close cropped grass that bordered the parking space.

"Boys, stop that, your clothes will be all green." They laughed and paid me no mind.

"I like green," Josh said with a giggle.

"Oh, you're hopeless," I said. Finally they tired and grabbed the food I laid out on the tailgate of the wagon.

Josh paused halfway through his sandwich while gazing up at the building. "Where's Mama's room?"

"On the opposite side, so I doubt that she can see us," Papa returned.

"I bet she'd like one of these sausage biscuits," George added, smacking his lips.

They all turned their gazes on me. "I thought of Mama." I answered the accusing stares. "Look," I said, lifting a smaller basket from the wagon. With the lid removed, I exposed the pile of fried apple pies. The warmth of the sun brought the spicy fragrance alive. "I got up early so I could make these. There's plenty for everyone, including Mama."

Papa's eyes gleamed when he looked at me, in wonder it seemed. "Come on," he said gruffly. "Finish your meal so we can take those pies up to your mother."

We trekked in single file up the winding narrow steps. They had put Mama on the second floor. "S-h-h-h, you kids be

The Chosen Child   *Joan Hall*

quiet, there's sick people in these rooms," Papa cautioned when a muffled moan of pain emanated through a closed door. Finally, we reached her room. A faded number 202 marred the door.

Papa rapped softly and an achingly familiar voice called, "Come in." In an easy chair by the window sat Mama. We couldn't miss the light in her eyes when she saw us kids.

"Mama, Mama." Arms hugged her and small pursed mouths placed kisses about her cheek.

A smile brightened her face. "Oh, it's so good to see you all." Tears clouded her eyes as she hugged first one child then another.

"Are you feeling better yet?" George asked, his expression pleading for an affirmative reply.

"Some times," Mama replied. "Yesterday I went outside and sat in the sun. There's a nice private area behind the hospital where patients can go. But I'm a little weak today." Mama's words halted as a spasm caught her chest. She turned her head away from the children and tried to stifle the cough, but failed. Her hands pushed at Becky who sat on her lap, so I lifted the baby into my arms. "It's probably best if you children don't get too close when I'm coughing," she said between gasps for breath.

"Don't wear your Mama out," Papa said as he reached

The Chosen Child   *Joan Hall*

out and took her hand. "She needs her strength to get well so we can take her home soon."

As I held Becky, I let my gaze wander about the small room. Painted grey with a grey tile floor, the area appeared dull and drab, even lifeless. Maybe that accounted for the tint of grey I noticed around my mother's mouth; her light skin absorbed the tone of the room. A narrow bed with white covers, a metal nightstand and the easy chair in which she sat encompassed the furnishings of the room. How could Mama stand to be cooped up in that small space? She had to get well soon and come back to our bright home with the tall slim windows that lit the rooms sunshine bright.

"The doctor started me on a medicine yesterday, some kind of sulfur stuff. He thinks it'll make me better." Her voice lifted with hope but she let her head fall back against the chair as if the weight was too much for her to carry.

I glanced down into the waste pail on the floor beside her chair. The towels she used to catch sputum were stained with blood. A sudden fear overwhelmed me, a fear that our mother was more ill than we realized. She needed good care and she needed strong prayers.

When tiredness tugged at Mama's eyelids, we said goodbye, each giving her a hug and kiss. Papa clung to her and she clung to him. I pushed the kids out the door so they could

The Chosen Child   *Joan Hall*

have a little time alone. After a few minutes Papa joined us on the main floor.

"Hold out your arms," he said to us, his voice tight and breathless. I had forgotten all about the skin tests the children and I had endured. My heart tripped as Papa scanned the outstretched arms, in a search for reaction. The scratches were still noticeable but no swelling or unnatural redness marked the spots. "I'm sure the nurse will agree that the rest of us are fine. But we'll have to check again for reaction in a few hours." His breath swept out of him in relief. "I guess it's about time we headed back home." We gathered the kids together and lifted them into the wagon. I hated the thought of leaving Mama in that awful room but we had to. My sisters and brothers were showing signs of tiredness. A least the ride home would be quieter since they were all worn out. It would be good to get them home and to bed. I had to concentrate on their well-being now. Mama was in the hands of the good doctors and of course, God.

Chapter Four

The next evening the kids were lined up for inspection. They each had the responsibility of bathing and dressing themselves, all except Becky. Taking what was normally my mother's position I walked by them, pausing in front of each to tuck a strand of hair or straighten a collar or remove a stubborn smudge of dirt. "Are we all ready to go to church?" I prodded each child with my eyes.

"Yes, Abby," they answered in unison.

"George, there will be no tugging of Lucy's hair while the members are praying." I scolded the most unruly of the trio

The Chosen Child   *Joan Hall*

of boys.

"How did you know about that?" George asked, an impish grin on his face.

"Never you mind how I know," I answered. "You just make sure you behave tonight, do you hear?"

"Okay," he grudgingly agreed.

"Now, when you get to church," I cautioned, "I want you all to sit quietly and when it comes time to pray, I want you all to pray really hard for Mama."

"We will," Lucy cried as she twisted a lock of auburn hair around a forefinger. Her strained face reflected the effect Mama's absence had on the family. The mainstay of our group was missing. Life had suddenly shown us its harsh side and rocked our secure world.

"Oh, we will," George added solemnly. "And I won't horse around either," he assured me.

"Mama, Mama." Becky began to cry again. I had been occupied all day with trying to pacify her. For the hundredth time I picked up the child and hugged her close. "S-h-h-h, baby, Mama will be home soon, s-h-h-h."

That evening the church overflowed with neighbors and friends. Heads turned to stare at my father with eyes full of sympathy. Word of our plight had evidently traveled fast. We filed up the center aisle, Papa first. He walked humbly with his

The Chosen Child   *Joan Hall*

hat in his hand. I followed close behind him with Becky astride my hip. Lucy and the boys trailed in single file. Ladies who were seated close to the center aisle reached out and patted me on the shoulder or the smaller children on the head.

"If there's anything we can do, just holler," a kindly lady said.

"I know this is mighty worrysome. If you need us, we'll be glad to help out," another whispered softly.

I smiled my thanks. I felt better already. The heavy ache in my heart grew lighter. Everything would be fine.

A rousing sermon ensued, befitting a first night of revival with Preacher Allison extolling the beauty of life as a Christian and explicitly describing the terrible fate of those who reject the Lord. His exuberance brought forth, "Hallelujahs," from throughout the building.

After the meeting, the preacher paused and wiped his brow then turned to my father and addressed him. "Brother Potter, don't despair, the Lord takes care of his own. In your darkest hour there will be a light." He clutched at his chest dramatically. "I can feel it in my heart. He will show you a way and make your burden easier to bear. Just put your trust in the Lord."

I turned my gaze upon my father. A hopeful expression brightened his face. He had needed to hear those words so

The Chosen Child   *Joan Hall*

badly.   Papa was sitting next to Luke so I couldn't help but notice him also. The expression on his face sent frightened chills up my spine.   Luke was staring at me and his eyes glistened and he had a half smile on his face. He licked his lips as he stared, not at my face, his gaze was lower. Slumping my shoulders forward, I made an effort to conceal my budding figure.   My face flushed crimson and I hung my head for I realized what the look meant. I couldn't help but know I was pretty, but the young men around had never given me such scrutiny. They stared sometimes but their eyes would be all soft and sometimes they blushed. I had stood proudly before them, but Luke made me wish I were a little girl again with a body like a slim reed.

"Now, let us pray." Preacher Allison lowered his head and the congregation followed suit. Desperately I tried to pray but the words just wouldn't come. My mind was too troubled. Finally I whispered, "Bless my family, Lord, and make my Mama well again, please." I was afraid to raise my head as usual for I could still feel Luke's eyes prying beneath my clothes, so I scooted lower in my seat.

After the prayer, Preacher Allison passed around the plate with a request for aid to our family. "Folks, you all know about poor Molly Potter's condition. I know you're not a wealthy lot, but please find it in your heart to help this family as

The Chosen Child   *Joan Hall*

much as you can. We all know how expensive doctors can be and every little bit helps."

I hadn't even thought about money. How was Papa ever going to pay for our mother's care? Silently he accepted the handful of crumpled bills. "I sure do thank you all," was all he managed to say before his voice choked off, his eyes misting with threatening tears.

"Could I talk to you in private, Ezra?" Luke walked up and placed his arm around Papa's shoulders, giving him a brotherly hug which seemed out of character.

I saw and rushed for the door with Becky in my arms. "We'll wait for you in the wagon, Papa." I didn't want to be near the man who made my insides churn with dislike. "Come on children, follow me," I said brusquely to my siblings.

A chilly wind had sprung up during the church service. The day had been hazy and hot with the hollows steeping and quiet, even the birds had ceased their singing, often a signal of an impending storm. The children sat huddled in the wagon, seeking comfort from one another. I chastised myself for not having the foresight to bring along a blanket. The horizon had turned a bluish black, thunder rumbled ominously in the distance and lightning slashed the heavens like the pattern in a broken window pane. I hugged Becky's warm little body close. With a feeling of impending disaster, I felt an urgency and

The Chosen Child   *Joan Hall*

uttered, "I'd better go get Papa cause it looks like we're in for a dreadful storm."

"Ezra, have you been thinking about what I asked you the other night?" Luke stood near the corner of the church house next to Papa.

"Abby is just too young for courting, Luke. You should call on a lady closer to your own age," Papa answered with his head downcast.

I stopped short just out of the light when I heard my name mentioned. I didn't believe my ears. Surely old Luke Johnson couldn't think Papa would allow him to call on me. He must be insane. Why, he was old enough to be my father's father.

Luke grew agitated at my father's resistance and raised his voice making it sound more nasal. "But it has been prophesied, Ezra."

"What do you mean?" Papa asked, seeming dumbstruck. "Prophesied?" he repeated, taking a step backwards away from Luke. He had to tip his head back to meet the taller man's eyes.

"I, I was praying in there about how to help my neighbor, and it just came to me, like a vision." Luke passed a hand before his face as if to illustrate what he had been privileged to see. His eyes grew large as if he were beholding a great scene and the sharp lines in his face softened. "It was just

The Chosen Child   *Joan Hall*

like the Lord touched me and I started to glow, like a light, and I knew what it meant. Abby has been chosen to fulfill the prophesy." He turned back to lock his gaze with my father's and put heavy emphasis on his next words. "I'm supposed to make your family my family. I am to be your guiding light." Luke tugged his hat down against the surge of tearing wind, covering his squinting eyes. "You believe in the power of the Lord, don't you, Ezra?"

"Of course I do," Papa replied in a defensive tone. He bowed like a young tree in the wind to the strong figure leaning over him.

"If I married Abby, you and Molly would be my family too, and I always take care of my family. I would see that Molly got the best of care," Luke explained. Papa didn't reply but stared with wide unblinking eyes. Luke acted encouraged. "It was meant to be, don't you see? The preacher saw it. You heard what he said about a light - well, I'm that light." Luke lifted his arms skyward and raised his face toward Heaven then brought his gaze back to Papa. "It was like a calling. I was told to marry Abby. It's God's will."

Papa stood hypnotized by Luke's compelling gaze. He clutched his thin jacket closer seeming unsure of himself. Did he think Luke was the answer to his prayers?

Luke would not relent and continued his tirade. "Don't

The Chosen Child   *Joan Hall*

deny God's will, Ezra, and make Molly suffer. I can take good care of your daughter. I carry the burden of the cross on my heart. I have to act. I have to do the will of God. I'll give Abby a good home and she won't have to work hard, just wifely things about the house. I'll make Molly well again just like God told me to do." Luke lifted his voice, rivaling the howling wind. He grabbed Papa by the arms and shook him. "God has given you a way and you can't refuse him. Molly's recovery is up to you."

Papa passed a trembling hand over his eyes, his expression full of doubt. Lifting his face upward, he pleaded aloud, "I don't know what to do. If you really told Luke to choose my Abby then give me a sign, Lord. Help me."

An explosion shot through the air so loud it burst inside my head and vibrated through my body. I stood frozen as a shattering blast crashed through the air just where Papa had been. My father lay on the ground stunned, seeming unable to move. Luke lay on the ground too with his arm thrown across Papa's chest. People gathered around, peering down at them. Luke was first to rise. He breathed heavily and he had lost his hat. His hair flew wildly about his piercing eyes. "Are you all right, Ezra?" he asked, peering down at Papa.

"Thank God you two are safe," a neighbor shouted as he helped the two shaken men to their feet.

The Chosen Child   *Joan Hall*

"Thank you, Lord." I almost sobbed in relief. Papa was alive. He rose and dusted off his clothes, staggering only slightly.

"Boy, that sure was close," another yelled. "That was mighty quick action, Luke. You saved Ezra's life for sure. That tree branch just missed him by a hair."

My father turned his shocked gaze to where he had been standing just seconds before. A giant limb lay smashed upon the ground. The huge oak tree that had been standing in the church yard for maybe a hundred years had been struck by lightning. Just at the moment when he had asked for a sign, and now I could tell that he believed.

"See," Luke grated, "He told me to take care of you."

Papa turned his head from Luke, as if he could not stand to look into his eyes, but yet hung onto him. Neighbors praised Luke for his quick actions. I felt an uncontrollable urge to cry. Something was terribly wrong, I decided, and hurried back to the wagon to wait for Papa.

He came moments later and jumped into the driver's seat pausing only long enough to glance over his brood. "We're fine," I answered his unasked question. The storm drew nearer and the sky grew more threatening as he urged the horses forward at a gallop. We had no more than a mile to travel and made it in record time, bouncing into the ruts and bumping over

The Chosen Child   *Joan Hall*

stones. Lucy and I huddled low, close behind our father but the boys shouted with excitement.

"Beat the storm, Papa, beat the storm."

The first big drops of rain pelted our heads as we scampered from the wagon to the protection of the snug warm house. The rain battered the walls relentlessly and beat a frantic rhythm on the tin roof. I sat the kids around the big oak table for some warm milk flavored with a spoonful of cocoa and sugar. I could not allow my gaze to meet Papa's eyes when he came inside after putting away the horses. With my head lowered, I handed him a cup of hot cocoa.

He pulled off his dripping jacket and hung it on a nail by the door. "Boy, that sure is some storm," he muttered as he took a sip from his cup. I couldn't find the words for a reply, afraid to encourage the conversation, afraid of where it might lead. I could hardly swallow my hot chocolate because tightness gripped my throat.

"Were you almost killed, Papa?" Lucy asked, her eyes round and glowing with reflected light from the kerosene lamp sitting in the center of the table.

When Papa nodded his head, George gave a nervous giggle and said, "I never thought old Luke could move so fast."

"He had power in him for sure." Papa turned to me and continued, "A woman would be mighty lucky to have a godly

The Chosen Child   *Joan Hall*

man like that."

"We're very thankful he saved you, Papa," I managed to say, and meant it too.

"Then you ought to tell him proper," my father said in a firm manner.

A premonition of what was coming next entered my mind and I didn't want to hear the words. I had to stop him from saying something he would be sorry for tomorrow. Jumping to my feet, I cried, "I'm tired, Papa, I think I'll go to bed. Lucy can help the younger ones tonight."

"Abby," he called as I left the room. "There's something important I want to discuss with you."

"Can't it wait until morning?" I wanted him to have time to think, time to change his mind. Surely by tomorrow he would see with a clearer head. He was still caught up in the drama of Luke's act of bravery tonight.

"All right." He sighed. "We'll talk tomorrow." He seemed relieved too.

Once I was snuggled comfortably in my familiar bed, I prayed, "Lord, please don't let Papa make me see Luke Johnson. He scares me so." Into the darkened room I cried aloud, "Please, please keep Luke away from me." A loud clap of thunder boomed. "I hope you can hear me above the storm, Lord," I whispered. "If Mama were only here, she would hit

The Chosen Child   *Joan Hall*

old Luke over the head with a rolling pin if he so much as looked at me, but Papa, Papa just isn't strong willed like Mama. He needs someone to lean on. Mama's not here now and poor Papa is so lost without her. Please let Mama come home soon, Amen." I wiped my wet cheeks and covered my ears to block out the worsening storm.

Chapter Five

Fragrant clover blossoms sweetened the morning air after the night's rain. Humming as I worked, I spread chopped corn for the chickens and gathered eggs from the hen house. This was my favorite time of day, when dawn was just breaking, the deadness of night being brought to life anew, like a rebirth. The rain had washed away the late summer dust that seemed to layer everything, leaving a newness that rivaled spring. A sparrow, perched on a nearby fence post, serenaded me with song. The bird appeared to be full of appreciation. I too, felt like singing in praise for mornings like this and little

The Chosen Child   *Joan Hall*

feathered friends with which to share them.

My light mood clung through the chore of getting breakfast. "Good morning, Papa," I caroled while placing salt cured bacon and scrambled eggs in front of him.

"You're awfully chipper this morning."

"It's such a beautiful day and I just have a good feeling." I sat down opposite him.

Papa smiled softly at me and said, "My first born, you always were a blithe child, always finding something to smile about, even in the worst of times." He had a reflective look in his eyes and let out a long breath. "Maybe that's why Luke Johnson finds you so charming."

I almost dropped my fork and the churning of dread renewed in my stomach. I had tried to forget the events of the night before. Papa cleared his throat and got right to the point. "Luke and I have been talking. He wants to marry you, and I said that he could."

A shudder seized me, making me choke on my food. His words struck me like a blow, knocking the breath from me. My whole world came crashing down. His words lodged somewhere deep within my chest forming an ache that consumed me. "Papa, you can't be serious; marry old Luke Johnson? Why, I can't stand him." I scoffed at the very idea. "He's old enough to be my grandfather, and he's mean, I know

The Chosen Child *Joan Hall*

he's mean, I can see it in his eyes." My troubled gaze searched my father's face. "Surely you don't believe the lies he told you." Sweat gathered in the palms of my hands and I rubbed them down my dress. I wished I could as easily rub away the hurt that Papa's words brought to my heart. "He scares me, Papa. Please don't make me marry him."

"I've already given my blessing, girl. He's coming by at ten o'clock to take you to town to get your blood tests." Papa lowered his eyes to stare at his plate and avoided meeting my pleading gaze. His jaw tightened in an unusually firm manner.

"I don't want to marry Luke," I cried. Desperation caused me to dare raise my voice in defiance. "I hate him. He's old and ugly. You can't make me. I won't. I would rather die first." Tears threatened just behind my lids. "How could you even suggest such a thing?" My dear Papa, whom I loved with all my heart was actually wanting, no, demanding that I marry that awful old man.

Papa slapped his hand down on the table with such force the dishes rattled and his coffee spilled on the clean white tablecloth. "It has to be, Abby. Luke had a vision at the church. It's God's will. The Lord chose you to be our instrument of salvation from this terrible trial. God told him to wed you and make us his family. God wants Luke to help take care of Molly."

The Chosen Child   *Joan Hall*

"Papa," I pleaded desperately, a helplessness growing inside me. "You can't believe Luke. This is only a scheme. He's an evil man with immoral thoughts. I can tell by the way he looks at me, he - he undresses me with his eyes."

"Don't say such things," Papa grated, his face growing livid. My words made him uncomfortable. He could not see his young daughter as the object of any man's lust. His eyes held an unnatural glare. "Luke is a fine God-fearing man. Besides, I asked for a sign and I got it. Luke saved me from that lightning strike as sure as my name is Potter, and that was proof enough for me. God spoke; I have to listen and obey"

Noting the stubborn sound of Papa's words, I decided to change my strategy. "Well, at least let me think about it. Luke can come and court me." I shuddered at the thought but I would do anything to keep from marrying him. Maybe I could bear his company for short visits if I had too.

"No!" A pulse throbbed in his temple and his eyes took on the appearance of a trapped animal. "There's no time for that, Molly needs care now." He rose from the table so suddenly that his chair crashed backward, hitting the floor with a loud crack.

"What has Mama got to do with this?" I asked, shocked at the turn of the conversation.

"Luke promised, as soon as the two of you are wed, he

The Chosen Child   *Joan Hall*

will give me money for Molly's expenses."

"You're selling me? How could you, how could you?" My world ended and my heart shredded into tiny pieces.

Raising his hand, Papa threatened to strike me. I had never before witnessed such anger in him. Suddenly he was a stranger. Gone was the soft spoken gentle man who had reared me. In his place was an alien driven by fear. Painful circumstance had robbed him of rational thought and reason. "Don't you say a thing like that. Luke will be family. He kindly offered his help and we need it. There's no room for Molly in the state sanatorium in Louisville. Her care is on my shoulders."

"But, but what about the money from the congregation?" I asked through numbed lips. "They gave us a whole handful of bills. Surely that will help."

"Twenty-seven dollars." He spread his hands out in a helpless gesture. "Do you know how far twenty-seven dollars is going to go?" Papa's eyes showed signs of desperation. "Do you realize how expensive your Mama's care is going to be?" He answered his own question. "It's going to take months, Abby, months or maybe even years, and I don't have any money. I've failed Molly. I can't take proper care of her without Luke."

"I could go to work," I volunteered, hope lifting my

The Chosen Child   *Joan Hall*

voice. "I could clean houses. The ladies in town pay good money if you work hard."

"It wouldn't be enough." Suddenly he slumped and dropped his head into his hands. His shoulders heaved with jerking spasms. A terrible noise erupted from him that tore at me. My Papa was crying. "I just can't stand to see Molly suffer and not get the proper medicine." Lifting his head he beseeched me with pleading eyes. "I can't let her die, Abby, I love her." He convulsed with a great sob that brought me to my knees beside him.

"Don't worry, Papa. Mama won't die. She'll be all right." I forgot my own misery; my only thought now was to console my father. "It's okay, I - I can grow to love Luke if it really is God's will, I'll marry him."

He wiped at his eyes. "You'll have a good life. Luke said you wouldn't have to work the fields, just take care of the house, just wifely things. He won't bother you much, cause he's old." Papa's face colored and he squirmed uncomfortably in his chair.

"I'm not even through school yet, Papa. I've got one more year before I get my certificate. You know how much it means to me to continue. I want to be something some day. I haven't decided yet what I want to do, but I know I need my education."

The Chosen Child   *Joan Hall*

"You've got eleven years of schooling." He argued. "That's a lot more than I had as a boy. It ought to be enough to get you by. It don't take book learning to run a house."

"What about the children? They need me now. Becky is just a baby and clings to me so." My voice took on a resigned tone. A sense of helplessness washed over me in devastating waves. I was losing the fight. My future was being laid out before me and it was not a bright picture.

Papa had a quick answer. He had evidently been pondering the situation. "Lucy will take over; after all, she's almost fourteen."

"But Lucy's awfully flighty and she never liked housework, and she daydreams a lot."

"Well, she will just have to get out of that nonsense. It's about time she grew up." Papa brightened, blew his nose, wiped at his eyes and straightened his shoulders. "Things are going to work out, aren't they, Abby?" The hope in his voice was almost a living entity. I felt I could reach out and grab it from the air.

He was the child and I, the elder. I patted him on the shoulder. "Yes, Papa, things will work out, don't worry." How could I not agree with him? Sighing heavily, I rose to my feet. The burden weighing on my shoulders made me stumble. My feet were wooden blocks that moved only with a concentrated

The Chosen Child   *Joan Hall*

effort. Sadness tore deeply into my soul leaving me feeling wounded and raw. I desperately needed to be alone for awhile. "I think I'll go for a walk. The children will be up shortly; their breakfast is ready and waiting on the stove. I'll be back soon."

I sauntered along the well trodden cow path that wound through the flat pasture, and up the hill behind the barn, drained of energy, will, even of life itself. I knew I must feel like someone who had just been told she was going to die, at first rejecting her fate, denying, angered by the news, and then, finally accepting her doom. I was doomed; no other word could describe my future. What a terrible choice - marrying Luke Johnson or letting my mother die for lack of medical care. No, actually, I had no choice at all. How could I live with my mother's death on my conscious? I couldn't. I loved her so much I would do anything for her, even marry Luke.

Upon topping the rise of the hill, I climbed through the rail fence into the orchard. The apples were just beginning to fall. It was time they were canned. Mama and I had intended to start next week. It had been a good year for apples. The limbs of the trees were so laden they swayed beneath the weight, some even touching the ground. Bounty enough for canning, drying, making apple butter, and jelly, and even a good supply for burying. We could hill up enough to have fresh crisp apples all winter long. I picked a Summer Scarlet and rubbed it

The Chosen Child   *Joan Hall*

against my dress until it shone then took a bite, grimacing at the tartness.

I sat down on an outcropping of sun-bleached rock near a patch of vines laden with blackberries that needed picking. A person could work from sun-up to sun-down in harvest season and still not get everything done. From my perch I could view the entire farm. I knew every acre by heart for I had spent my entire life here. Lost Creek cut a path around our property. My gaze followed the river's path as far as my eyes could see. It disappeared around the bend of Laurel Hollow in the direction of Luke's property. I had never ventured that far up the long meandering valley. Five other tracks lay before Luke's boundary began near the head of the hollow, where the mountains met and formed a ridge. Having heard about his big two story house, with its ten rooms and electric lights, perched at the base of the area's tallest mountain, I had been mildly curious. But now, I dreaded the time I would lay eyes on it.

Turning my gaze to our front yard, I stared at the swing hanging from the oak tree. Papa had built it for me when I was about five years old. Now I had to leave it all, my home and my family, to live with that scary old man. An explosive anguish began building inside me. Suddenly, it burst forth in a piercing wail. I screamed, like I did when I was a child with a tantrum, my useless cry bouncing back to taunt me as an echo. I threw myself down on the ground and beat at it helplessly with my fists. "No, no, no." There wasn't any one to hear, so I shrieked until exhaustion claimed me, and my throat ached, then I lay quietly in the grass in numbed acceptance.

I lifted my head when the sunshine grew uncomfortably warm on my back. Shading my eyes with my hand, I checked the sun's position in the sky. I realized it was probably ten o'clock, or maybe later. The sky mocked me with a clear blue open space, almost breathtaking in beauty. It had no right to be so lovely on a day like today. Dark angry clouds should be rolling and churning, or a scowl of dark grayness would befit my mood. I rose to my feet and listlessly traced my path back down the hill. Luke's car sat in the lane next to the house, a big black monster with silver eyes and silver teeth, waiting to gobble me up.

When I opened the back screen door, Lucy met me with disbelieving eyes. "Is it true? Are you really going to marry old Luke Johnson?" I nodded my head.

"Why, Abby, why?"

"There are some things you're simply too young to understand, Lucy."

"Ugh." She gagged and held her stomach, doubling over in mock distress.

"That's exactly how I feel about it too." I choked on the

The Chosen Child   *Joan Hall*

words.

"Well, I'll never understand this, no matter how old I get. I think you're crazy." Lucy sucked in her breath and pressed her hand against her mouth. Pity poured forth from her eyes. She tagged behind me to the washstand. "Don't do this, Abby. I don't know what Luke is putting over on Papa, but it can't be worth this. You've been crying, haven't you?" She reached out and gently touched the puffy tissue beneath my eyes. "Just tell Papa you won't do it and that's that." She stomped her foot and folded her arms across her chest.

I realized I hadn't given my younger sister credit; hadn't seen how astute she really was. "I can't tell you all the details, but I have to marry him. I really have no choice," I said, my voice dead. I gave Lucy a forced smile, then hurriedly washed my face, and smoothed my hair, before stepping into the living room. Luke sat on the sofa with his dress felt hat in his hands. When he spotted me, he pushed himself to his feet. Papa stood close by the door, and after a furtive glance in my direction, made a quick exit without speaking.

"Are you ready to go, Abby?" I didn't answer, I couldn't. Never would I be ready to marry him. Luke smiled. I noticed he was missing a tooth, and the rest were stained from tobacco use. At my brief nod, we walked outside. He opened the car door for me and I hesitated.

The Chosen Child   *Joan Hall*

Glancing over my shoulder, I gave one last pleading call, "Papa."

No answer returned, so Luke nudged me in the back. "Get in," he said impatiently. With a shuddering breath, I climbed through the gaping hole, into the black monster. We rode in silence until reaching the main road. The operation of the vehicle held a strange fascination, and the noise of the engine roared in my ears. I had never ridden in a car before, and found it more comfortable than I had imagined.

"I'll teach you how to drive this thing, if you like." Luke was the first to speak, his voice gravelly. My skin crawled.

"No thank you." I occupied myself by staring out of the window, and counting the fence posts as they whizzed by. I tried not to think or to feel.

"This is for the best, Abby. This is what God wanted to happen." I pretended not to hear. "I had a vision," he said in awed reverence. "You were chosen." Turning, I stared coldly at him and his words faltered.

Shaking my head in anger, the wispy ringlets around my face bounced, tickling my face. "I am not like my Papa who's easily fooled. I know what you did. You blackmailed him. If I was chosen, it was only by you. God would not do such a thing. You knew just what to say, didn't you?" If I was going

The Chosen Child   *Joan Hall*

to my death I might as well go bravely.

Luke gripped the steering wheel until his knuckles turned white. Dropping all pretense of fulfilling the Lord's will, his mouth pulled down at the corners and he spoke in a rock hard voice. "Yes, but the facts are Ezra needs me, and Molly needs me, and I want you. It seems like a fair deal to me."

Staring closely at him, I noted small beads of sweat on his wrinkled forehead, and he had nicked himself shaving. I could even see tiny blotches of purplish veins marching across his face like an army of spiders. "How can I be sure you'll keep your end of the bargain?"

"I gave my word, and Luke Johnson always keeps his word." He spoke emphatically without taking his eyes from the road, but he lifted his chin. So far he had proved himself to be cunning and evil, even using the Lord in his schemes. I couldn't let him cheat on his part of the deal. I had to make sure I didn't suffer this fate in vain.

Luke made plans for the wedding with my resigned acceptance, and had me back at the house by noon. The ceremony would be performed by Preacher Allison after the regular service on Friday night, three days away. Just three more days of freedom unless a miracle happened, and the way my luck was running, I wasn't about to hold my breath.

I thought and planned all afternoon, then at supper time,

The Chosen Child   *Joan Hall*

I asked Papa, "How much money will it take to make Mama well?"

He raked his fingers through his hair. "I have no idea, Abby. It all depends on how long she'll be sick. It may be six months or a year or two years. Tuberculosis is not something you can get cured right away. The expense will be much less if Molly can get admitted to the sanitarium, but until then, it's mighty expensive."

"But can't you make a guess?" I needed a general figure. "Two hundred? Five hundred?"

He gave a biting half-laugh and grunted, "With the doctors and medicine and her room, it will be more like five thousand."

"Five thousand." My hand fluttered to my chest. That seemed like all the money in the world. *Could Luke Johnson possibly have that much money?*

"What made you ask that?" He peered at me with puzzled eyes that made me squirm.

"I was just wondering," I replied, making an effort to keep my voice calm despite the turmoil in my head.

How could three days have passed so quickly? I supposed it was because I had stayed so busy, hardly allowing myself time to think or feel. Lucy and I canned fruits and

The Chosen Child   *Joan Hall*

vegetables every day. I wanted to put away as much food as possible for the family before I had to leave. Lucy was just learning and still did only what she was told. How would she ever cope with the responsibility that was soon to be put on her? She would just have to, just like I had to marry Luke.

The Chosen Child   *Joan Hall*

Chapter Six

For the hundredth time I smoothed my hands down my best Sunday dress. It was my only white one, a cotton eyelet with a red ribbon sash made with store bought fabric. The short sleeves billowed full to the elbow and the waistline held almost two yards of gathers. I knew because I made the dress myself. Luke was to pick me up to take me to the church. Papa and the children had already left. Nervously, I peeked out the window when I heard the car roar up the lane. After long moments a knock sounded at the door. Swallowing to moisten my dry throat, I called out, "Come in."

The Chosen Child   *Joan Hall*

Luke stepped through the doorway wearing a navy suit and a black tie. The clothes were old fashioned but he did appear better looking than usual. He clutched a new tan hat in his hands. For a moment he just stood there without speaking, seeming unsure of himself. After clearing his throat he said, "Let's go, Abby."

"Not yet," I answered firmly although my heart thumped warily in my chest. "First there's something we have to do." I had dared challenge him, and had to follow through with my plan.

Luke looked blankly at me as I handed him a folded piece of paper and a pen. "What's this?" he growled, regaining the composure that was his usual nature.

"I want you to write Papa an IOU for four thousand dollars to be paid over the next two years and then sign him a check for one thousand dollars." Standing bravely, I braced my hands on my hips and held my breath. Would he actually sign over so much money to marry me? Perhaps I had asked for too much, but I needed enough to assure my mother's care. I could settle for no less.

Luke's face slowly turned a mottled red. "Are you crazy, girl?" he flared. "Do you realize how much money that is?" He strode back and forth in front of me, shaking the paper like it was burning his fingers. "I said I would take care of

The Chosen Child   *Joan Hall*

Molly's expenses, and I meant it. Me and Ezra have already come to an agreement."

"Well, then marry Papa," I stated in a calm voice. "You have your conditions. You either sign the papers or leave, without me." I plopped myself down on the sofa. I wasn't going anywhere.

"Now don't go getting stubborn," he coaxed. "You don't want to disobey your Papa, now do you?" I would not play the helpless child he thought me to be.

"If I'm old enough to get married, then I'm old enough to make up my own mind and it has been made up." I hoped I had not pushed him too far.

Luke stared at me, his eyes moving up and down my slim body while he pondered the situation. If he dared resist, he would have to drag me kicking and screaming into the church and I was sure he knew that by my defiant words. Restlessly he ran his fingers through his hair, and then he turned and gazed out the window, then pivoted back toward me. If he didn't respond, could I deny my father and refuse this marriage. Doubt seized me. What if Luke didn't have this much money or maybe he would have been as good as his word and paid for Mama's expenses. No, all my intuition told me this was the way to be sure. I had to follow through. He shouldn't mind if he was planning to give Papa the money anyway.

The Chosen Child   *Joan Hall*

"All right, if that's the way it's gotta be," he said, reaching for the pen and paper. My breath escaped slowly in a sigh of relief.

I looked at the note, making sure it was written correctly. "Now, the check."

Luke jerked out his checkbook with a loud, "Hrump," and quickly filled it in. "Now are you ready to go to the church?" he demanded, slamming his hat onto his head.

"Not just yet," I answered. "You go on to the car; I'll follow in a minute." Watching from the window, I saw him climb behind the wheel and slam the car door behind him. Where could I hide the valuable papers so they would be safe? The cupboard was too obvious. Under the mattress? No, that would be the first place Luke would look if he tried to back out of the deal. I ran over and turned back the corner of the worn linoleum rug, and placed my cache between it and the floor. No one would think of checking there, and I would tell Papa as soon as possible, so he could put the check in the bank. Now, I was ready to go to the church and marry Luke Johnson.

The congregation stood with hymn books in hand, their voices wailing the rolling rhythm of Amazing Grace. Meekly, I followed Luke down the aisle of the church. I thought our entrance might go unnoticed amid the vehemence of song, but was mistaken. It seemed everyone turned to stare at me, but

The Chosen Child   *Joan Hall*

there was no faltering of voices.

My eyes caught and locked with the gaze of Mrs. Warden. Pity radiated from the woman's open round face. I knew what she was thinking. It wasn't so unusual for a man of Luke's age to take a young wife but she was sorry that I would never know the rapture of young love like she and her dear husband had experienced. I would never be held in the arms of a strong youthful lover who would awaken and share the newness of physical love with me. Luke was no longer that man. Age had caused his once wide shoulders to droop, and his long definite stride had become a shuffling of feet.

"I once was lost but now I'm found,

Was blind but now I see."

The haunting melody echoed through my numbed brain. I loved the refrain. Often my mother had rocked a child to sleep singing the words. Normally, I found peace when I heard the song. An uncomfortable ache formed in my throat, and I hurriedly blinked my eyes. I must not think of my mother. Purposely I cleared my mind of any thought. It was better to be like an unliving thing with no feeling, like the podium on which Preacher Allison leaned. I had to get through the service, and the ceremony without crying. How would it look if I broke down? Standing with my head downcast, I stared at the floor. I began counting the nails that held the rough plank flooring in place. When that was done, I moved my gaze to the wood grains of the oak pew in front of me. The circles and swirls of wood took shape, becoming ghoulish faces that taunted me, wretched expressions of torment from gaping mouths and sagging folds of skin. On the verge of hysteria, I squeezed my eyes tightly closed. When the song ended, I gratefully dropped into a seat. Luke sat on my left and on my right was Doyle and next was Edward. Rescuing me from the imagined tormentors, Doyle nudged me in the side with his elbow and snickered, "Are you going to be my new Ma, Abby?"

"Yes," I hissed, anger bringing life back into my numb body, "and the first thing I'm going to do is take a strap to you."

His lean young body shook with laughter. He assumed a relaxed pose, stretching his long denim clad legs out in front of him, crossed at the ankles. "Don't you think twenty-three is a little old for a strapping?" he needled, giving me a side glance from shuttered eyes.

I turned cool blue eyes on him. "I could have sworn you were a smart mouth kid."

Doyle's eyes flashed anger in return. "We'll see who the kid is. I'll teach you a thing or two, just you wait and see."

"Shut-up, Doyle." Edward reached over and poked his brother. "Leave her be." He had been slumped in his seat, unmindful it seemed, of the bantering between us. His eyes met

The Chosen Child   *Joan Hall*

mine, and there was sympathy in his gaze. At least there would be someone in the household on my side. Edward winked at me, and I found a small reason to smile. During the rest of the service I sat in silence. Preacher Allison's sermon was about loving thy neighbor as thyself. It appeared to me that a plot had been formed to push me into Luke Johnson's clutches.

"Now, we have a special occasion tonight. It is my honor to join Luke Johnson and Abigail Lee Potter in holy wedlock." The preacher beamed as he held out his hands and beckoned the two of us forward, toward the altar. Silently I screamed, *Oh Papa, please save me, don't let this happen, help me, please.* The seconds ticked endlessly. A silence fell throughout the congregation. All I could hear was the ragged breath of the man standing so close to me.

We stood before the altar as the preacher thumbed through his Bible, searching for the proper verse to begin the ceremony. He took his time while giving me furtive looks, giving me ample time for a last minute change of heart. *No, Preacher, I won't back out, I can't.* I lifted my chin and met Preacher Allison's gaze. "Luke Johnson, do you take Abigail Lee Potter to be your lawfully . . ." My surroundings faded as thoughts raced through my head, overwhelming me. Maybe this was not really happening. I would soon wake up in my soft feather bed.

The Chosen Child   *Joan Hall*

"Hey, Lucy," I would call across the room as my sister stretched and rubbed the sleep from her eyes. "I just had the most awful dream and it seemed so real. I was marrying Luke Johnson. Can you imagine that?"

Lucy would sit up in her bed and giggle. "That is the most ridiculous dream you have ever had, Abby - marrying old Luke."

"I know," I would reply. "I could never marry him in a million years."

"A trillion years," Lucy would return, falling back on her bed in a fit of laughter.

Luke grabbed me by the arm, forcing my attention back to the ceremony. He rasped under his breath, "Answer him, Abby."

Startled, I looked up into the preacher's smiling expectant face and uttered a barely audible, "I do." Was that trembling voice mine? Had I actually become Luke's wife? This wasn't a dream, it was a nightmare, a living nightmare and it was just beginning. As I turned, my glazed eyes met Papa's. Doubt clouded his gaze. He seemed to be asking me if he had done the right thing. He lifted his hand as if to object, but instead, slowly lowered it to his side, where it dangled lifelessly.

I gave him a forced smile. It was too late for regret

The Chosen Child   *Joan Hall*

now; the deed was done. My father was worried enough about Mama, he didn't need suffer the pain of remorse as well. "It's all right, Papa," I whispered toward him as I walked down the aisle beside my new husband, then out of the church.

I surely didn't feel like celebrating the event but custom demanded a party in the shelter house. We walked the few feet to where an area had been cleared of grass and flat creek rock had been laid as a floor. A tin roof supported by barn poles completed the structure. In minutes we were surrounded by the church members. Local musicians had brought their instruments in preparation, a guitar, banjo and fiddle. Everyone gathered in a circle while the musicians tuned their strings, leaving an open space for the bride and groom to begin the dance. Finally the plunking sounds of Po' Black Sheep bounced through the evening air. Hands clapped and feet stomped in time. How fitting a tune, I thought. I felt like a poor little lamb, but more like one led to the slaughter.

"Come on Luke, swing that little bride."

"Yeah, Luke."

"Folks, make way for the bride and groom."

"Abby, go dance with your new husband." A woman standing near prodded me. Luke's arm slide around my waist and pulled me toward center stage. Normally I loved music and dance, with my feet acting almost of their own free will, but

The Chosen Child   *Joan Hall*

now my posture remained stiff and my feet moved woodenly. I counted the rises and falls of the tune anticipating the end. Finally the tempo switched to another melody and the others anxiously crowded the floor. A sigh escaped me as the attention shifted from me and Luke. We edged our way through the throng to the side. Luke leaned down and whispered close to my ear, "Now's a good time to leave. They're too busy to miss us. The boys have already left for home." My heart tripped. I was leaving the safety of the gathering. Luke grabbed my hand and pulled me after him.

Abruptly, the chiming of the mantle clock in the next room brought me back to the present - my wedding night. The timepiece struck ten times.

Luke still stood across the bedroom, his ragged breathing the only sound in the room. Finally, he called out, "Come here girl."

With each frightened step, whimpers emanated from my lips, sounding like the cries of a puppy. Against my will, I moved to where his words throbbed out of the darkness. Hesitantly I placed one foot in front of the other, until I was close enough to feel his harsh wheezing breath. He grabbed me and jerked me down onto the bed with him. I lost my breath as he rolled me over and climbed on top of me. Luke groaned and covered my mouth with his. A small cry burst from my lips as I

The Chosen Child   *Joan Hall*

gasped for air. His weight held me down and the liquor on his breath brought nausea closer. Helplessly I fought him. The searing violation happened quickly yet my pain would be eternal. Weakness washed over me in swirling waves and I felt myself sinking into a deep space then being enveloped in blackness. When Luke rolled off me, I was barely conscious.

With my last ounce of strength, I pulled my hurting body to the edge of the bed as the world spun around me. Never had I suspected I would hurt so much. Was this what sex was all about? This union was supposed to cement a marriage and make two people as one. I had been cheated. Never would I experience love like I had read about in many of my books. I was doomed to a life of being handled and abused but never loved, a life of hell on earth. Tears coursed silently down my cheeks. Savagely, I had been striped of my dreams.

"I hate you, Luke Johnson," I ground beneath my breath. My thoughts then swept to my father. *You betrayed me, Papa, you betrayed me. How could you have sentenced me to this prison?* Desperately I gripped the edge of the mattress, as far from Luke as I could get. Chills shook my body, so I grasped the corner of a blanket and pulled it up over myself. A cruel thing had just happened to me. I was really married to Luke Johnson.

Tonight would not be a night of peaceful sleep.

The Chosen Child   *Joan Hall*

Unfamiliar and very disturbing emotions churned inside me and frightened me, almost as much as Luke did. Never had I experienced this awful feeling of hatred. It was a distasteful thing that threatened to consume me and I sought to expel it from my mind.

My bruised body ached as I tossed to my side. The blackness of the night cloaked the unfamiliar room and the man lying beside me in the bed. Reluctantly, I closed my tired eyes and willed my uneasy mind to cease its restlessness. A long sigh escaped me and finally, exhaustion demanded that I succumb to the numbness of sleep.

Chapter Seven

In spite of the long, frightful night, I awoke as usual at the stroke of six. Slowly, I turned my head to stare at the man whose bed I shared. The shame of last night washed over me anew. I steeled myself against the emotions that wanted to break loose. I would not cry again, but rise and face my new life. Nothing could match the horror I had already endured.

Luke lay on his back with his mouth agape, snoring loudly. He seemed harmless in that pose. Sleep had relaxed the scowl he usually wore, and softened the harsh lines about his mouth. He didn't appear to be the monster I knew him to be.

The Chosen Child   *Joan Hall*

Slipping quietly off the bed, I hoped not to wake him. I couldn't stand to be touched again this morning. The air was already warm, hinting at the heat the day would later bring.

Hurriedly I twisted my hair atop my head in order to feel as cool as possible. By the early morning light, I stared at my reflection in the dresser mirror. My eyes were puffy, my face pale and my figure drawn, but I knew the resilience of my young body. I would recover quickly and I would learn to carry this horrible burden of married life. My book, Heidi, teased me with its presence. Quietly, I picked up the novel and rubbed my hand over the brown frayed cover. The innocence of the text haunted me. I slipped open the bureau drawer and placed the book beneath my clothing. I had lost my connection to the girl on the pages.

Stillness lay throughout the house. I tiptoed around in fear of rousing someone. It was good to be alone. I would like to be alone forever or at least a couple of hours while the men slept. With a deep breath I stretched my sore muscles. I must have lain in a tight position all night. My hands itched to clean the filthy house, but first there was something that had to be done.

"Come here, doggie, come here." I tried to entice the hound from her comfortable bed by calling softly, but had no success. When I held a chunk of raw bacon in front of her, she did lift her head and sniff, but dropped back onto her paws and closed her eyes. "You lazy thing," I cried in a hushed voice. "You're too lazy even to eat." I grabbed her by the collar and tugged the dog's resistant body toward the door. Whining her objection, the animal braced her paws and scooted along on the floor. "From now on, you sleep in the yard," I said as I gave her behind a final push out the doorway.

Soon I had the potent aroma of coffee filling the kitchen. "That sure does smell good," said a deep appreciative voice. I jumped at the sudden appearance behind me.

"Edward, you frightened me." My trembling hand fluttered to my chest where I clutched at my dress just over my pounding heart.

"Sorry," he apologized. "I was sitting on the back porch watching the sunrise then I smelled the coffee." Without his cap, his dark hair was still rumpled from sleep. He appeared more boy than his manly eighteen years. His figure was too lean, almost gaunt in his faded chambray shirt and worn bibs. A woman's cooking would fill him out, I decided.

"I love the sunrise too," I exclaimed. "Here." I handed him a steaming cup of coffee. Edward gratefully took the mug, nodded his thanks, and turned back toward the door.

"Do you mind if I join you?"

"No, I don't mind at all," he answered, sounding

The Chosen Child   *Joan Hall*

pleased. He held the screen door open wide for me. I dropped down on the wooden steps while Edward sat down in the only rocking chair. We stared in silence as the sun climbed gloriously over the eastern tree line. It emblazoned the sky with brilliant fire. Orange and red rays burst forth, streaming through the lacy edges of tree leaves to catch us in the glow, until it seemed we were in the center of a bright sphere. The scene held me spellbound until Edward spoke.

"A red sky in the morning means bad weather is coming," he said a hint of uneasiness in his voice.

"Yes, but it's still a beautiful sight. How can anything so lovely be a bad omen?" I leaned back against a post and breathed a sigh. The sun's healing warmth eased my sore body, seemed even to touch my bruised soul.

"Maybe God tempered the bad with a little good." Edward pushed his dark locks back to rest his hand on his forehead, shading his eyes as he stared moodily into the distant sky. "I think God does that a lot." His words puzzled me and I gave him a quizzical stare, so he continued. "You know," he prodded, giving me a restless glance. "Like mushrooms, some are good to eat and others will kill you. And a shimmering deep pool of water, in spite of all its good uses, you can drown in the midst of its beauty." He hesitated and cleared his throat as if what he was about to say made him uncomfortable.

The Chosen Child   *Joan Hall*

Moving restlessly in his chair, he said, "People are like that too, you know, none of us is perfect. One may seem bad, but there will be a little good in him, and somebody who is good will have a little bit of bad in him, also."

"I never thought about it but I suppose you might be right, Edward. My Papa is a good man but he has his weaknesses," I admitted. I was pretty sure he was trying to tell me to find the goodness in his father, and decided I would try, but I knew I would have to search awfully hard.

"What time do Luke and Doyle usually get up? I'll have breakfast waiting."

"It'll be awhile yet. I'm the only early riser around here. I take care of the morning chores." Edward took a long sip of coffee and carelessly crossed his legs.

"But what about the crops? This is the busiest time of the year."

"Oh, don't worry." Edward averted his eyes. "The work will get done." Hurriedly, he changed the subject. "Why don't we eat then just keep breakfast warm for them."

"All right, I've got a lot of work to do today, and I'd like to get started." After locating the makings of a hearty meal - sausage and eggs and plenty of flour for biscuits, I began cooking.

When Edward sat down to the fare placed before him,

his eyes widened. He propped his elbows on the red-checked tablecloth and stared at his plate. "Gee, that sure looks good, Abby. A man gets mighty tired of his own cooking." He dove into his food with the appreciation that only an eighteen-year-old could muster.

I ate sparingly. My appetite had disappeared but I knew I needed to keep up my strength so I forced down a few bites. Edward wandered back outside after he had consumed everything on his plate, and I began the chore of cleaning the kitchen. Everywhere I looked, was a thick layer of grease and soot. As I worked, I kept checking the clock. Seven came, then eight, finally at nine o'clock, when the kitchen was sparkling clean, Doyle came stumbling in.

As he advanced, he ran a hand through his shock of tan hair. A stubble of beard shadowed his angular face. "Is Pa up yet?" He pulled out a chair and dropped into it. Propping his elbows on the table, he held his chin with both hands, and slowly allowed his gaze to rove over me, from head to toe.

He hadn't bothered to give me a proper morning greeting and uneasiness grew within me. "No, just Edward."

His eyes took on an odd, unreadable expression and a half smile played at his mouth, no, not a smile, more like a smirk. "You sure did surprise everybody."

"Oh?" I didn't know how to respond to his baited

The Chosen Child   *Joan Hall*

statement although I knew he was referring to mine and Luke's quick wedding.

"Marrying my Pa - so sudden like." When I didn't respond, his eyes flashed and the corners of his mouth drew down in a sneer. "Yeah, you sure pulled a fast one. I can't blame my Pa though, you being so pretty and all."

"You - you don't understand, Doyle." I hesitated, searching for the words to explain my actions, shocked at the depth of his spitefulness. How dare he put me on the defensive, suggesting that I preyed upon his father and snared him in a trap.

"Well, make me understand," he demanded, his face a sullen mask. "Tell me why you did it."

I struggled to find the words. "Luke . . . Luke had a vision at the church and Papa believed him and . . . and . . ." I couldn't go on. The pain was too new and deep to be shared with anyone, especially the likes of this arrogant hateful youth.

"And what?" Doyle demanded. His dark brows gathered together over familiar piercing squinty eyes. The way he looked at me made me feel like a meatless bone and he a ravenous gnawing dog.

"You will just have to ask your Pa." Turning, I fled to the other side of the room to busy myself at the stove. I would not hear any more. This marriage was not my idea; it was all

The Chosen Child *Joan Hall*

Luke's scheme. I longed to give vent to my resentment and blurt out the real reason, his father's lust.

Before I could gather enough nerve to speak, Doyle's young voice lowered to an angry growl. "I don't have to ask. Everybody knows my Pa has money and you intend to get it, don't you?" He leaned forward in his chair and spread his hands on the table assuming the manner of a crouching animal. He put more emphasis on his words, throwing them at me like stones to bruise my flesh. "Well, that money belongs to all us Johnsons and ain't no pretty girl gonna get her hands on any of it."

Standing in shocked silence, I received a crash course in growing up. No one had ever spoken to me in such a manner. Never again would I feel like the coddled child. Remembering the money stashed under the rug at Papa's house, guilt coursed through me, so I clamped my mouth tightly on the hurtful words that were on the tip of my tongue. I was as much to blame as anyone. Perhaps I could have made my father understand. I had to admit to myself that once I learned of the dire straits my parents were in, I had wanted Luke's money, but only for my mother's sake, never for my own.

"Morning." Luke came shuffling into the room, buttoning his shirt as he walked. "Smells good in here," he said, drawing a deep breath into his lungs and slapping his hand against his chest. "It's mighty nice to have a woman around this house again."

Doyle snickered and peered at me from the corners of his eyes, his anger of a few moments earlier cleverly hidden by a more jovial manner. "I guess you could call Abby a woman this morning." Heat flushed my cheeks crimson. Luke cuffed Doyle lightly on the head in mock rebuff, but he wore a wide grin on his face.

"You keep a civil tongue in your head, son. I don't want you showing no disrespect to my new wife." As I placed the food on the table in silence, I grew conscious of Doyle's hateful eyes following me.

"Doyle, I think you had better go after some supplies today. Try Vanceburg, you haven't been that way for awhile." Luke paused and took a bite from a fluffy biscuit. "M-m-m," He closed his eyes in appreciation. "Oh yeah," he reminded himself of the statement he had begun. "We got a sale lined up for that last, uh, crop of corn."

Doyle jerked upright in his chair and stared at Luke as if he had lost his mind. Nervously, he rubbed his knuckles in the palm of his other hand. "But Pa, I thought we were just going to store the grain away for awhile - until the market clears. Now is just not the right time." His gaze flew to me as if he were uncomfortable speaking about business in front of a woman. He hushed, but I got the impression that he would like to have said more.

"Things have changed," Luke muttered between mouthfuls. "I don't think we have anything to worry about." His voice rang firm and sure. Doyle started to object, but Luke held up a hand stopping him. "I don't want no back talk, son. Do you hear? I've been overseeing this operation for many a year without any trouble. I know what I'm doing."

"You'd better be right, old man," Doyle said reluctantly, giving his father a rebellious stare from beneath a scowling brow.

It was another hour before the men left the house and climbed into Luke's car. After waiting another fifteen minutes, I slipped off my apron. No one was in sight when I slipped out to the barn. Inside a stall, I found a handsome red mare. I walked close and touched my fingers to her head, all the while speaking soothing words to the animal. "There, there, girl, aren't you a beautiful thing; you have such a shiny coat." I found a bridle hanging on a nail close by. "Will you let me ride you?" I asked in a soft voice as I rubbed my hand down her side. The mare nodded her head as if understanding my request, so I gently placed the halter over the horse's head, and then, with the aid of a block of wood on which to step, mounted the animal. The mare showed no rejection of my slight weight on

The Chosen Child *Joan Hall*

her back, so I urged her through the stall door and out of the barn.

Everything appeared the same as I rode up the lane to Papa's house. Somehow I had expected it all to be changed - as I was. The boys were chasing each other around the yard as if they had nothing better to do. They should be having lunch now. My father always liked to eat at eleven-thirty sharp.

Utter chaos greeted me when I entered the house. Becky sat in the middle of the kitchen floor screaming, her tiny face puffy and red from an evidently lengthy bout of crying. Smoke swirled around the top of the room like a storm cloud from the burned food on the stove. Lucy was scraping blackened fried potatoes from an iron skillet. Her face was flushed to the color of baked candied apples by heat and frustration, and her hair, which was cut in comely bangs, clung wetly to her forehead. She turned in desperation when she heard my entry.

"Am I glad to see you," she wailed, appearing close to tears. "Nothing is going right without you, Abby. Becky hasn't hushed all morning, the boys won't mind me and the stove got too hot and burned the food." Lucy wiped her hand across her eyes as a sob broke through. Her voice teemed with ragged emotion. "Why did you have to leave, Abby? We need you here."

I picked up Becky and hugged her close. The baby

The Chosen Child   *Joan Hall*

hushed immediately in the familiar embrace. I swung her back and forth, all the while crooning to her. Within seconds the exhausted child fell asleep on my shoulder. "Has she had her nap?" I asked in an accusing voice, frowning my disapproval at Lucy.

"She wouldn't take her nap," Lucy complained in her child-like voice. "All she's done is cry, cry, cry."

I carried the sleeping infant into a bedroom, and gently lay her on the bed. Lucy was waiting when I came back into the kitchen. She held a defiant stance, a spatula in one hand and a dishtowel hanging from the other.

"I just can't handle this, Abby. I'm at my wits end." Her lip stuck out in a pout as she flung the dishcloth onto a counter.

Staring at my younger sister, I recalled that when I was Lucy's age I was already handling most of the household chores. Our mother was feeling poorly even then, and I, as the oldest was expected to be the responsible one. I hadn't minded, but realized now that Lucy should have shared the load. She would have been better prepared for the current circumstance.

"Now, Lucy," I soothed in a calm voice, "get a hold of yourself, things aren't too bad. It just seems difficult because this is your first day. It will get easier, you'll see. Oh," I added on a long quivering breath, "where's Papa?"

The Chosen Child   *Joan Hall*

"He's waiting on the back porch. I was late with his lunch - and now I've burned it."

"There are brown beans in the ice box from yesterday. You can warm them up right quick. They will go great with your cornbread. I'll slice some fresh tomatoes over lettuce." My years of coping with the demands of my family gave me the skill of changing turmoil to order. Hurriedly I set the table and called everyone to eat.

Papa's shoulders seemed more stooped than usual, and there were deep recesses around his eyes. My heart ached when he looked at me and asked, "Are you all right, daughter?" There was a definite break in his voice. His second thoughts had come too late.

"Yes, Papa, I'm fine." I smiled and the realization struck me that I didn't hate him after all. I could never feel hate toward someone I loved so much. Circumstance had ruled his actions. Desperate people do desperate things, I reasoned.

The boys came tearing in, a mass of flailing arms and stomping feet. George halted and clutched dramatically at his throat. "A-h-h-h, we can't eat in here with all this smoke." He gagged and choked, all the while laughing. "I can't even breathe."

Papa swatted him on the seat of his ragged pants, causing a puff of dust to billow around him. "Stop your making

The Chosen Child   *Joan Hall*

fun. I think Lucy did right well. Look how yellow her cornbread is, and its all golden brown on the top." Lucy broke into a smile and Paul giggled as George rubbed his stinging behind. Suddenly we all burst out laughing, and it was almost as it used to be - almost.

When we had finished eating, I hurried into the living room. The papers were still tucked beneath the rug where I had stashed them the previous evening. "Here, Papa." Eagerly I pushed the notes into his hand. As he peered at the crumpled documents, his eyes questioned me. Watching closely, I noted how his chin dropped and his eyes widened. He broke into a wide smile, erasing some of the hurt that had tortured his handsome face for the last several days. I would marry Luke all over again if it would make Papa that happy.

"Abby, this here's a check for a thousand dollars. I can't believe it."

"Yes, I know." I pulled myself up to my tallest. "Now, Mama can get the best of care. Maybe you can even buy her a treat the next time you visit."

"That's an awful lot of money." Papa frowned and his gaze searched deep into my eyes. "How come Luke is giving me so much money so soon - and this IOU." He fingered the papers and shuffled his feet on the floor as he always did when he became nervous. "It just don't seem right."

The Chosen Child   *Joan Hall*

Hurriedly, I tried to explain and reassure him. "Luke just wanted to show you he meant what he said. It was done in good faith - really. Shucks, that's not a lot of money to Luke." I couldn't help but smile at the relief on his face, but I hastened to caution him. "You go directly and deposit that check in the bank and put that IOU in a safe place too. It wouldn't do to lose them."

"I'll go as soon as I can saddle Homer." Papa rushed toward the door. He stepped higher than he had in a long time and a flush brightened his face. "I knew we did the right thing, Abby. You marrying Luke was the answer to a prayer."

"So that's why you married that old coot," Lucy said as soon as the door closed behind our father's back. "I still don't like it and I'm afraid for you, but I understand." Lucy put her arms around my neck and squeezed real hard. "Thank you, Abby, for helping Mama. I'll try harder to do my part." As she pulled away from me, tears glistened in her eyes.

"I'd better get back to the Johnson's - I mean home," I corrected myself.

"Will you come again tomorrow?" she begged. "I miss you."

"I don't think I can, but I'll come again soon." I swallowed around the lump in my throat. It hurt me to say those words. Lucy needed a little freedom to grow, without me. She would become more confident in her new role, and I was sure Luke would not react well to my visits if he discovered them.

Chapter Eight

The trip had taken nearly two hours. There was no sign of Luke's car as I led the mare back into the barn. Thank goodness no one would know I had been gone. Relieved, I felt I could afford a few minutes to rub down the animal. I worked in silence except to make comforting sounds to reassure the mare. The animal had taken to me, obeying each soft spoken command. The horse turned to gaze at me with wide appealing eyes. "You are a good one, aren't you, girl." I patted her affectionately on the forehead, and the horse nudged me in return. "I like you too," I laughed, and hugged the animal's neck.

The sudden crunch of gravel and the drone of male voices startled me. I hadn't heard the men coming, and now they were just outside the barn door. Surely I would be spotted if I dashed for the house. Without thinking, I scurried up a nearby ladder, and barely had time to bury myself in a pile of hay in the barn loft. Peeking through a crack in the loft floor, I saw Luke and Doyle enter the barn. They were arguing heatedly, their bodies stiffened with tension.

"I'm the one taking all the risks," Doyle hissed, as he slammed a fist into a timber directly below where I lay. I had never witnessed such anger and my heart jumped in fright. "I tell you, Pa, the Rameys know what they're talking about, and they say it's getting hot. There were two strange fellows asking questions around town last week; I'm afraid the law is on to us." Doyle's voice rose until he shouted so loudly my ears rang with each word.

They stood in dark silhouette against the backdrop of sunshine streaming through the barn door. Nearly the same height and weight, they faced each other squarely. "And I say you're just getting scared," Luke growled back, shaking his finger in his son's face. "I know what I'm doing. There's no way that stuff can be traced to us. It's always been cash in hand; nary a paper has ever been signed. They would have to

The Chosen Child   *Joan Hall*

catch us red handed. All we do is make it, the distribution is left up to the other fellows. They're the ones taking the risks."

"Yeah, but I'm the one running the stuff to the sellers. I got no hankering to spend time in the pen. I say we lay low for awhile till them fellows leave. We got enough money stashed in the bank to last us for a mighty long spell."

At the mention of money, Luke fell silent. He pulled the hat from his head, and wiped the perspiration from his brow on the sleeve of his blue shirt. "I had to use a little of that money, son."

"For what?" Doyle's eyes darkened. He stopped his pacing to stand before his father with his hands balled into tightened fists at his sides, displaying a willingness to fight to the death. He advanced closer to his father, the intimidation obvious.

Luke moved back a step to scrutinize his son. I had never seen him so unsure of himself. He had seemed to always overpower anyone in his company. It was he who was always right, with no apologies. "I gave Ezra a check - to help with Molly's expenses."

"You did what?" A low snarl tore free from Doyle's throat. "You gave our money to Ezra Potter? How much did you give him?"

"A thousand dollars." Luke raised his voice in defiance.

The Chosen Child   *Joan Hall*

"A thousand dollars," Doyle repeated, in a disbelieving tone. He raised a hand and punched a finger to Luke's chest in a threatening manner. "You just up and gave away a thousand dollars after I risked my neck to earn it?"

"It's my money too," Luke blustered, "and I can spend my share any way I like, besides, there's plenty more where that came from."

"You can spend your part but you're sure as hell not going to give it away." Doyle stood in front of his father, his stance rigid. Cowering, I burrowed deeper into the cover of hay.

Doyle slapped his hand against his forehead as realization struck him. "It's Abby, ain't it? You paid for her like you would a sack of flour. No wonder this marriage happened so quick-like."

"That's not the way it was," Luke denied, his voice wavering slightly. "I'm just helping Ezra out. He's in a real fix with Molly needing medical help."

"Since when did you get so charitable?" Doyle sneered. "Just how much helping out do you intend to do with our money?" Doyle put heavy emphasis on his last two words, his eyes blazing. Luke didn't answer, and Doyle grabbed him by the front of his shirt, jerking him close. "How much?" he demanded through clenched teeth.

"Four . . . four thousand dollars," Luke stammered. "It was the only way Abby would go through with the wedding. If she hadn't rebelled I could have strung Ezra along."

I knew it; I knew the crook wouldn't keep his end of the bargain.

Doyle staggered when he heard the sum his father uttered, falling speechless for a moment. His voice grew steely hard. "Well, since you bought Abby with our money, I'll just see that I get my part of her too."

A gasp burst from me, and then I caught my breath, hoping I hadn't been heard. His words cut through me with the keenness of a razor. I needn't have worried, the two men were not conscious of anything except their anger and each other.

"You keep your hands off my wife, do you hear? She's mine, we spoke the vows together and no man can put that asunder." Luke's large hands curled into fists like his son's.

"Was she worth it?" Doyle laughed. "Don't tell me, I'll find out for myself."

An angry growl began down deep inside Luke and came out as a snarl. "You touch Abby and I'll . . ." He was so worked up, his face twitched uncontrollably and his body jerked as if he were a puppet and someone was pulling the strings.

"You'll what?" Doyle challenged his father with a smirking face. "You're old, Pa, too old for a young girl like

The Chosen Child   *Joan Hall*

Abby. Maybe it's time I started running things around here."
Doyle threw back his shoulders in an act of bravado and gave
his trousers a tug at the waist. "I'll take over the operation and
I'll see to Abby too."

Luke had been pushed too far. He jerked the hat from
his head and threw it aside. "Looks like you need a licking,
son. I'm going to put you in your place. You'll still answer to
me as long as I'm alive."

Doyle laughed wildly. "We'll just see who is the better
man, and who will do the answering." The two men faced each
other like opposing male animals. Luke stepped around Doyle,
eyeing him closely, searching for a weak point before making
his move. Doyle lunged at Luke before he could act and they
both crashed to the ground. Quickly they rose again to their feet.
Could Luke ever compete with his younger and stronger son?
Muscles rippled beneath Doyle's plaid shirt as he flexed his
arms in preparation to do battle, but Luke was taller and carried
more weight and he was more experienced in such things as
fighting, so maybe he had a chance.

Dust swirled around the pair. Doyle flashed out a fist
and Luke cried out and crashed to the ground. Instead of trying
to rise to his feet, Luke stuck out his legs, catching his son in a
vice-like grip. He jerked, bringing Doyle into a coiled twist.
They grabbed each other at the same time and began wrestling,

The Chosen Child *Joan Hall*

rolling and twisting in the dirt. I could not see who was on top, but recognized Doyle's laughter and the grunts were definitely Luke's. I covered my ears to block out the sound of fists slamming flesh. Curses growled between clenched teeth as the two thrashed about.

"Damn you, old man. I'm gonna kill you."

"You'll wish I was dead before I get through with you. I brung you into this world and I can take you out."

"Oh yeah?"

"Yeah."

Finally, after long moments of warring, an arm drew back a tight fist, hesitated, then plummeted downward. A loud crack echoed through the barn and one figure lay still. Slowly the victor got to his feet. I caught my breath because the winner held my fate in his hands. Luke stood unsteadily, his chest heaving. He bent forward to rest his hands against his legs in an attempt to catch his breath.

"Maybe next time you'll think twice before you challenge your Pa," he said to the limp figure lying sprawled unconscious on the dirt floor. He stepped across the still body of his son to retrieve his hat, then turned and headed down the lane toward the creek. He stepped proudly, with his shoulders thrown back like a cocky rooster, still ruler of the roost.

Weak with relief, I decided there were fates worse than

The Chosen Child   *Joan Hall*

Luke Johnson. After waiting long moments, until Luke was out
of sight, I climbed down from my hiding place. I jumped over
Doyle's senseless form, and dashed for the relative safety of the
house.

That evening, as I readied myself for bed, my mind kept
reviewing the scene in the barn. Guilt gnawed at me. I never
intended to cause trouble between Luke and his sons, would
never have bargained for the money if Mama hadn't been in
such dire need. Besides, Luke was the first to mention money,
otherwise neither I nor Papa would have even thought of the
possibility. It was not my fault, I told myself.

How could life get so complicated? Was it only a week
ago that I was an innocent child, loving everything and
everyone in my sheltered life? Now I was caught in a trap of
my own making. Even though it was with the best of
intentions, it was I who built it, I who stood in front of the
preacher and said, "I do."

The trap was strong. How would I survive? On one
side was Luke with his clutching hands and greedy eyes, on
another was Doyle, who felt he owned a part of me and was just
waiting like a poised cat to make his move. The last side of the
trap was Edward. Maybe he was a weak point in the snare.
Edward viewed his family through forgiving eyes, but I felt he
had a soft spot for me as well. If I hovered close to him,

The Chosen Child   *Joan Hall*

perhaps I would be safer, I certainly would be more at ease. Edward, although strangely aloof, was the only member of my new family who didn't make my nerves tighten with fear. I pulled a deep shuddering breath. I would have to learn to be a wary animal if I were to survive.

At supper time, I couldn't help but note Doyle's reddened, bruised eyes and sullen expression. "What - what happened to your face?" I asked, pretending innocent curiosity.

Luke spoke, not allowing Doyle time to reply. "He just got too big for his britches, that's all, figured he could best his old man. Well, I showed him." Luke's eyes glittered triumphantly, and he chuckled as he bragged. "The only way he'll beat me is to gun me down or stick a knife in my gut."

The throttled violence between the two men was almost a palpable thing and I wanted it appeased. "The two of you shouldn't fight; after all, you're father and son."

"Life ain't sugar coated, Abby," Luke cautioned. "It's only human nature to have conflict and the strong will rule the weak. Now don't you worry no more about it." I considered his words. He thought of everyone but himself as weak and thus to be ruled by him. Silently, I vowed I would not be ruled by Luke Johnson.

A sudden burst of thunder rumbled like the growl of a giant angry beast. I was reminded of a book I had read once;

The Chosen Child   *Joan Hall*

about an ancient tribe of people who bowed to the maddened god of thunder, and offered him sacrifices to appease his violent nature. I could understand how those unlearned people could be frightened by the ominous roar especially when it boomed so loudly that the very earth on which they existed trembled.

Lightning still flashed as I lay down on my side of the bed for the night. I pulled up my knees and hugged myself in search of comfort.

"Are you afraid of the storm, Abby?" Luke raised up on one elbow, and peered at me through the darkness. "You can lie closer to me if you're a mind to."

"No, I'm fine where I am. I don't mind bad weather," I stammered. I wasn't afraid of the storm, just filled with a sense of dread, not because of the squall, more like a feeling of impending doom. With a shake of my head, I made an effort to rid myself of the fears. Luke reached out and brushed the hair away from my flushed face. I clenched my teeth in preparation of the act that was to come.

The night had grown sticky warm and I felt smothered, so I kicked the cotton sheet to the bottom of the bed. Luke lay snoring, unmindful of the insufferable heat. He had fallen asleep immediately after taking his privilege with me. Finding it impossible to sleep, I tossed for what seemed hours, until I

The Chosen Child *Joan Hall*

could stand it no longer and rose. Silently, I crept through the house and out the front door. It was slightly cooler outside and I detected a faint breeze. A full moon cast a soft glow and stars winked playfully although there were still occasional rumblings and flashes of heat lightning. The storm had passed without releasing a drop of rain. A shower would have cooled the air and been more than welcome.

I dropped down on the porch floor close to the edge where a rambling rose vine clung precariously to the boards. The vine wandered across the porch to a support post which it encircled with a profusion of tiny branches loaded with round plump wine colored rose buds. I reached out and plucked one, careful of the thorns. As I brought it to my face, I breathed deeply, drawing the sweet essence into me. These had been Chloe's pride and joy, according to Edward. She had always kept a vase of the blooms on her dining table while they were in bloom. I decided to honor Chloe's memory by brightening the table at tomorrow's evening meal as she had done. Edward would like that.

Through the part in my faded gown, I ran my hand over my tender breasts. This second night with Luke had been easier; at least it hadn't hurt quite as much as the night before. Did women actually enjoy this thing that happened between the sexes? Could love make a difference? Could this same act

The Chosen Child   *Joan Hall*

bring joy and delight instead of pain and such sense of dread? I guessed I would never know. An errant breeze crept beneath the loosened frock and caressed my bruised flesh. With my eyes closed, I dropped my head back so my sweeping hair would fall away from my damp neck.

From out of the darkness behind me flashed a callused hand that closed over my mouth as another hand grabbed me around the waist. Panic numbed my body and I gasped silently for breath as I scratched desperately at the gripping hands. My heart thumped like it might burst through my chest. Though I struggled, jerking and straining my body, I seemed powerless against the strength of the muscular arms gripping me. Effortlessly, the arms hauled me against a rock hard body and dragged me off the porch and into the blackness of the night shadows. Images flashed before my eyes, pictures of my brothers and sisters lying safely tucked in their beds and Luke stretched out, sleeping soundly just on the other side of the wall. Was this to be my end, so soon in life? The viciousness of the tearing hands told me my very life was at stake. My mind cried out in desperation. I could not die now, not like this, not when I was needed so much. "Lord, dear Lord, save me."

Terror renewed my strength and I dug my heels into the soft earth. I would not be an easy victim. I was surprisingly strong for my size and stature. The aggressor grunted against

The Chosen Child   *Joan Hall*

the strain of my resistance. My nostrils burned from the stench of hard liquor on the breath wheezed so close to my face. The grasping hand allowed only a muffled moan to emerge.

A loud yelp of pain shattered the night. The grip on me broke as my attacker fell to the ground, pulling me down on top of him and the snarling, biting hound dog that had been lying unnoticed in the shadows. I found an advantage and quickly rolled free of the tangle of flailing arms, hairy paws and bared canine teeth. I clamored back to the relative safety of the porch.

A wrenching human cry of pain followed me then a loud thump as the poor animal was slammed against the side of the house. A whimper from the dog followed, and then all was still again. I stumbled inside and quickly slipped the bolt that locked the door. My fingers shook so; it seemed to take an eternity to move the small round cylinder into place. The disturbance must have awakened someone upstairs, because a light flashed on and cast a yellow beam into the yard below. Through the small window of the door, I spied a tall lean figure hurrying toward the barn. He loped at a haphazard gait as if he were injured.

I turned and fell weakly against the door. I'd had a close call and would have to be more wary. There could never be any more nocturnal stirring like I had enjoyed in my youth, for someone skulked about under the cover of darkness, someone with evil in his heart. I hadn't been able to see the face of my attacker but my intuition told me that Doyle was the culprit.

Thank goodness the hound had chosen to sleep close by the house. I would definitely be more appreciative of the animal in the future. I had never really cared for hounds, considered them to be men's dogs, used to hunt down helpless critters in the woods. I preferred a dog that was more companion than hunter. I would have to ask Edward for the dog's name. The animal would hold a special place in my heart forevermore. Tomorrow, I would give her a bone, a choice bone with meat on it. Sudden exhaustion consumed me, weakening my knees, so I dragged myself back into Luke's bedroom and collapsed beside my soundly sleeping husband.

Chapter Nine

The next days passed in a blur of sameness. I did my household chores and at night suffered the passion of my husband, remaining at his side throughout the night, not daring to leave the bed lest Doyle lie in wait for me. I had made another hurried secretive trip back to my family's home and found things going a little more smoothly. Papa reported Mama's condition as much the same, but that she looked lovely in the new dressing gown he had taken her. I stared at the calendar hanging near the kitchen door. The days of my marriage now numbered eight. Restlessness wrecked my insides. I decided a stroll would lift my spirit. Since my chores were completed, I felt free to explore.

"Come here, Belle," I called to my new best friend, the hound who had rescued me that evening of my terrifying encounter on the porch. I learned Edward had given the dog her name.

"When the dog was just a tiny pup, she came running every time Ma rang the dinner bell. So I named her Belle," he had explained.

"Crazy name for a hunting dog," Luke had said in a derisive voice.

"I was just a boy then," Edward had added, not looking at his father.

Belle trotted along at my side. I slid my hand over the white tufted tops of the Queen Ann's Lace that grew wild along side the path. "Aren't these flowers beautiful, Belle? I'll gather a bouquet when we return and put them on the supper table." I leaned over and sniffed the fragrant lavender-colored blooms of the Milkweed but was careful not to touch the sticky plant. It was mid-afternoon and the temperature had climbed to a muggy ninety two degrees. Each day of August brought the temperature higher and higher. A break had to come soon. I slipped off my shoes and wiggled my toes. My senses awakened when I walked with my exposed skin upon the earth,

The Chosen Child   *Joan Hall*

feeling each texture. I kicked as I stepped through the warm sand. Sparkling grains shot upward to shower tiny jewels over the tops of my feet. The greatest pleasure though came from walking upon the thick carpet of moss that cushioned and quieted my steps when wandering within the forest.

Lost in thought, I had strayed a good distance from the house. From where I stood, it appeared so far away as to look like a tiny doll house, a nice pretend little house with a happy pretend family. "Stop this foolish nonsense," I scolded myself. "You're a grown woman now, a married woman. The house is real and you're too old for dolls."

I turned my attention to what lay before me. I was at the edge of the woods that covered the mountain on Luke's property. The temptation to venture up the hill was too great to resist. The leaves of the trees formed a canopy overhead, creating inviting shadows underneath.

"Come on, girl," I urged the hound to follow. As we stepped into the shade, I let out my breath on a sigh. The temperature was much cooler, I gave in to temptation and sat down on a rock and closed my eyes in pleasure. Belle was a quiet companion. Stillness surrounded me except for the sounds of the woods, the slight breeze ruffling the leaves, birds twittering, a woodpecker furiously rapping on a tree and a rustle in the brush. I peered uneasily toward the sound but saw

The Chosen Child *Joan Hall*

nothing. Probably just a harmless snake, I reassured herself.

The uneasy feeling lingered reminding me of my terrifying evening encounter on the porch. I had eyed carefully both Doyle and Edward as they each came to breakfast that morning after. I detected a slight limp in Doyle's gait reaffirming my suspicion that it was he who attacked me and struggled with the hound. Edward walked in slow deliberate steps but I dismissed him as a suspect. I couldn't imagine him assaulting anyone. Doyle had a surly expression for both Luke and me and had barely spoken, but he did wolf down the fare placed before him. Edward had been quiet as usual, but I caught him staring at me a couple of times with an unreadable expression on his face.

But now, for awhile, I was free - free of snide remarks and cruel stares and free of worry. For awhile, I would not think of my weak mother or unhappy father or of Luke and his clutching arms or Doyle's threats.

I jumped to my feet and spun around in delight and stretched my hands toward the incline. "This is a magical mountain and I am a princess who will explore it in search of . . ." What would I look for? The fountain of youth? No. A burning bush, like Moses found? No. My young mind searched. "I am a princess, so I will search for my prince, a handsome young man on a white steed to carry me away, a

The Chosen Child   *Joan Hall*

magical prince whose kiss will whisk away all the bad things in my world."

Where would a prince hide? I tiptoed up to a giant oak tree and peeked around the massive trunk. Perhaps he would be in the deeper forest higher on the mountain. A deer path wound through the underbrush and I decided I would follow, with Belle tagging behind, and see where it led me.

The trail twisted upward, not ending until it topped a plateau about halfway up the mountain. It had been a steep climb and even though it had been shaded most of the way, the exertion warmed my cheeks. As I paused to wipe the perspiration from my brow, I scoffed. My prince would not be here, not near these patches of thorny blackberry bushes. He would much prefer the leafy sprays of wild fern, and thick cushion of cool green moss that lay deeper within the forest.

I parted my way through a crop of mountain laurel, gasping at the vision on the other side. An immense pond of crystal water sparkled in the spattered sunlight. A natural spring sprouted from the earth where the hill continued upward, bubbling forth with eternal energy feeding the lake. I stooped and dipped my hand in the cool depths and brought the water to my hot cheeks. Belle lapped thirstily, and then sauntered over to lie in the shade.

My search for my imaginary prince was forgotten. I

The Chosen Child   *Joan Hall*

glanced around quickly, noting no living thing in sight. Hurriedly, I slipped my dress over my head and lay it neatly on a rock, then my slip, leaving me modestly covered by my cotton underwear. As I pulled the pins from my hair, the strands fell down my back. After another furtive peek around, I dove into the cool water. A delicious chill swept over me and I caught my breath, then burst into laughter that echoed back to my ears. I splashed and swam until I grew tired, then closed my eyes and floated in the center of the pond. The sun bestowed warm kisses on my skin where my body broke through the water.

Once I had rested, I dove beneath the surface and aimed my form in a smooth glide toward shore. My head came up out of the water as my feet touched bottom. With my hands, I brushed my hair from my face and blinked the wetness from my lashes. I froze at the sound of a masculine chuckle. Standing directly in front of me was a tall lean young man about six feet in height with wide shoulders. He wore tight fitting dungarees and a cream colored knit shirt. He stood in a casual pose with one hand on his hip and the other gripping a shotgun that rested with the stalk upon the bank. He had light blue eyes, a slim face with high defined cheekbones and a chiseled jaw. His hair was the color of honey.

I jerked my arms up and folded them across my wet bosom, outlined by my clinging undergarment. I tried to speak.

The Chosen Child   *Joan Hall*

My throat had suddenly grown numb with surprise. Finally, anger restored my voice and I cried, "Who are you? How dare you spy on me. This is private property and you have no right to be here."

"Whoa, whoa." The blond stranger held up his hand to halt my onslaught of words. "I just stumbled on to you - purely by accident. How was I to know that the splashing I heard was made by a beautiful maid. I assure you, I was expecting to bag a fine deer. That's why I advanced so quietly."

His words rang in my ears, "Beautiful maid." Words a prince might use. With a shake of my foolish head, I said, "You can't hunt on this property. It's posted; there are signs everywhere."

"Joshua Gaines gave me permission to hunt anywhere I please on his land," the laughing handsome face replied.

"But this isn't Gains property," I mimicked his teasing manner. "It belongs to Luke Johnson and you're trespassing." I placed my hands defiantly on my hips.

The young man's face flushed, and he dropped his eyes. Realizing what I had done, I stepped back, deeper into the cover of water. He was the first to break the silence that ensued with an attempt at lightness. "I do believe my lady is shy - and modest. I'll gladly turn my head so that you might clothe yourself."

The Chosen Child   *Joan Hall*

"Oh no, I don't trust you," I replied. "You could easily turn and peep."

"And risk your wrath?" he asked, laughing. "I think not."

"I want you to leave, completely out of sight."

"But then you couldn't know if I peeked or not. I could easily gaze upon you from the cover of the bush. This way, you could make sure I am turned from you."

The stranger made sense, it seemed. "All right, turn around," I agreed. He did as he was told and hesitantly I waded toward the bank. I tugged my clothes on as quickly as my trembling hands could pull the protesting cloth over my wet body. In seconds, the chore was done but it seemed like endless minutes. "Okay, I'm decent."

The young man turned appraising warm eyes on me and I blushed. "I never knew Luke Johnson had a daughter, let alone one as lovely as you."

"I'm not Luke's daughter, I'm Abigail . . ."

"Oh," he interrupted before I could finish. "You're Abigail Potter. I've heard of you. You're just as beautiful as they said you were." Heat flushed my cheeks at his compliment.

"Who told you about me?"

"Mr. and Mrs. Marcum. I'm staying in a room above

The Chosen Child   *Joan Hall*

their store. Nice folks." He laughed, a virile, youthful sound. "If this isn't Gaines property, that means you're trespassing too." He held out his hand to me. "It seems we have something in common, Abigail. My name is Christopher Barton, but you can call me Chris."

"You can call me Abby," I returned. "Everybody else does."

Chris smiled. "Why do parents give you long names, then immediately shorten them?"

I didn't reply, just mutely placed my hand in his extended one. Mine was enveloped by his firm grip. I felt small and fragile. His fingers were smooth, not rough like a farmer's hand. He did not toil in the fields, that was sure. There was another certainty too. Chris was a stranger to the area. His speech was precise and clipped, not slow and rolling like the locals. He was from somewhere up north, I was sure.

"Where are you from?" I asked pointedly.

He hesitated, and then replied, "I live in northern Virginia. I'll only be around for a few days. This is supposed to be a mighty good hunting area." He reached for my other hand and pulled me over to a huge slab of white limestone that jutted from the earth, making a natural shelf. He sat down on the smooth surface, and then motioned me to sit beside him.

My hair was beginning to dry around my face, becoming

The Chosen Child   *Joan Hall*

troublesome wisps that I tried unsuccessfully to tuck behind my ears. Chris smiled at my efforts. Our eyes met and he was a stranger no longer. His eyes were kind and gentle and I could have stared into their clear blue depths forever. No hidden leers made me turn away. I returned his smile freely.

"Luke Johnson won't like you being on his property," Chris warned. "I've heard he's a mean man." Concern creased his forehead and drew his blond brows together over soft heavy-lidded eyes.

I dropped my head. At the mention of Luke's name, reality came flooding back with a vengeance, bringing the sting of tears to my eyes. "No, I don't think he'll mind," I answered quietly.

Chris reached out his hand and cupped my chin, lifting my flooded eyes to meet his. "Why not?" he asked. "From what I hear everyone steers clear of the whole Johnson clan."

"Because - because I'm one of them," I said, ashamed at having to admit to such an association.

"But you just said you weren't his daughter."

"I'm not Luke's daughter, I'm his wife."

Chris reeled as if he had taken a blow to the chin, dropping my hand like he had been burned. "Why - why did you marry him?" His eyes held disbelief. "You can't be in love with him, he's old and cruel."

The Chosen Child   *Joan Hall*

"No, I don't love him, in fact I despise him."

Chris waited for me to say more and suddenly it was like a dam broke. I burst forth my misery, telling him everything about my mother's illness, Papa's weakness and his contract with Luke. I even dared to tell him about the close call I had on the porch. My hands shook as I recounted the experience. The words poured from me like water in a stream and I was powerless to stop them, like all the hurt and fear demanded a release. "I'm very frightened, Chris. I don't know where to turn. Edward is the only one I think I can trust."

"You can trust me." He took my trembling hand.

"Yes, I think I can trust you," I said as our eyes met. "But you're just a visitor. You'll soon be gone, and I'll still be a prisoner at Luke's mercy."

"You could leave him, Abby" Chris urged, his voice tense.

"No, I can't. I took a vow - for better or worse." I was almost sobbing.

"But it was under duress," he argued. "You don't have a real marriage. A union should be based on love."

"My mother needs the money. I can't let her down."

"All right, but maybe I can think of something."

"No," I hushed him and sighed. "There's nothing to be done. I made my bed so I have to lie in it, but thank you for

The Chosen Child   *Joan Hall*

your sympathy." Our eyes met again and a kinship was born, an understanding that denied the newness of our relationship.

I took a deep breath and asked, "Do you have brothers or sisters?" He had learned so much about me, yet I knew little about him.

"One sister, Beth."

"It would seem odd to have only one sibling," I said, thinking of my own large family.

We continued to talk, each revealing experiences of our youth. Chris had a privileged upbringing with a healthy mother and a father who worked daily in a factory. Our common bond was that love abounded in each of our homes. I was beginning to feel as if I had known him all my life.

"My family would like you," Chris said, his voice comforting me like a downy pillow.

"They sound nice," I returned.

Chris leaned his head forward and slowly, cautiously claimed my lips with his. The touch was light and breathless. My breath caught at the sweet sensation swelling my heart and sending a weakness rushing through my arms and legs. My mouth clung to his, not wanting the bliss to end.

Finally, reluctantly, he lifted his mouth away, but lingered close for a few seconds, his breath feathering my flushed cheek. "I'm sorry, I know I had no right to do that, but I

The Chosen Child   *Joan Hall*

just couldn't seem to help myself," he whispered.

I felt no guilt. Perhaps it would come later, but now there was no room for any other feeling but the warmth that filled me so completely. As I pulled away from Chris, I became aware of the lengthening shadows. A shudder jolted my body for the day had slipped away. I had been too lost in the joy of Chris's company.

"I must get back to the house. Luke will be home soon." Hurriedly, I twisted my hair up on my head. "Come on, Belle." I urged the hound away from the pine needle bed she had made. "Goodbye, Chris."

"Will you come again tomorrow?" he asked, hope lighting his eyes, "Please."

"I can't, Chris. It isn't right. If Luke found out . . ."

"He won't find out," Chris said. "We have just become friends. I want to get to know you better."

Now I understood what the word temptation meant. I could just hear Preacher Allison. "Temptation is a bad thing, a foul thing, oh, but it is sweet. The body will hunger for its delicious nectar, but after the feast comes the bitter aftertaste of shame." I envisioned the preacher with his eyebrows drawn together in anger and his finger pointed directly at me.

"No, no, I can't see you ever again. I - I have to go now," I cried, stumbling away from him. Just once, I turned

The Chosen Child   *Joan Hall*

and peeked over my shoulder at the tall, handsome prince who magically entered my desolate life, and gave me a brief glance at the joy that could lie in the relationship between a man and woman. Now, whenever things got too bad, I would just recall him and his touch and I would feel better.

When the dog and I stepped from the shadows of the woods into the late afternoon sun, I placed my hand up to shade my eyes and better see the house in the distance. My stomach curled in dread, for Luke's car sat in the lane. How could I have been so thoughtless, and how could time have passed so quickly. Lately, it had hung weighty upon my shoulders, making me glance often at the clock and wonder at how long a day could be. I rushed through the weeds and briars, unmindful of the scratches to my bare legs. As I hurried up the lane I did take time to grab a handful of Queen Ann's Lace to adorn the table.

"A-b-b-b-y." Luke's throaty call echoed off the distant hills.

Cupping a hand around the side of my mouth, I answered him. "I'm coming, Luke, I'm here."

He stood in an angry stance with his hands balled into tight fists at his sides, his face a mottled red. "Where the devil have you been?" Belle whined and tucked her tail between her legs then trotted away, leaving me to face Luke alone.

The Chosen Child   *Joan Hall*

Meekly, I stood in front of him, my chest heaving from my hurried steps. Looking him directly in the eye, I said, "I went for a walk. My chores were completed and I got restless."

"Nobody gave you permission to go snooping around." He grabbed me roughly by the arm. A tearing pain ripped to my shoulder bringing a cry to my lips.

"I - I wasn't snooping," I gasped.

"Where did you go? What did you do?"

"I didn't do anything." Luke didn't lessen his grip, so I added, "Water - I found a pond - I went swimming to cool off, that's all, I swear." Luke abruptly let go, causing me to stagger. Tears stung my eyes as I grabbed my hurting arm, but I wouldn't let them flow.

"Looks like I'm going to have to teach you a lesson, girl." Luke began unfastening his belt, and I watched in disbelief. I had never been struck before and froze in fear.

"No, please don't hit me, Luke."

"From now on, you ask permission before you take liberties. Your place is in the house and don't you forget it." Luke's eyes burned with anger as he raised the folded belt above his head. Turning my back, I squeezed my eyes tightly closed in dread. For long seconds I held my breath, and then a flash of fire struck my shoulders and brought me to my knees. As I went down my face got buried in the white fluffy flowers I

The Chosen Child   *Joan Hall*

clutched.

The thud of running feet penetrated the pain laced fog in my head. "Pa, Pa, have you lost your mind?" I lifted my gaze to see Edward pulling at Luke's upraised arm. His young face was frozen with horror.

Luke's eyes danced wildly under a thunderous brow, reminding me of the raging bull Papa kept in his back field. I had been warned not to go near the animal for fear of my life. "Let go of me," Luke stormed at his son. "A wife has to learn to be obedient to her husband. Obey - that's what the Bible says. Just like a child - spare the rod . . ." Luke's words rambled senselessly. Edward grabbed him by the shoulders and shook him hard.

"Pa - Pa, get a hold of yourself." Luke hushed and dropped his hands, allowing the leather strap to dangle at his side. He quieted but his shoulders heaved with labored breathing.

"Now, what's this all about?" Edward's dark eyes flashed first to Luke then to me where I still hovered on my knees.

"I came home and Abby wasn't in the house," Luke gasped his words. "I - I looked everywhere, I searched the house - the barn. I yelled for her and there was no answer."

Edward turned a beseeching gaze to me, and I cried, "I

The Chosen Child   *Joan Hall*

just went for a walk, that's all." I sputtered and wiped at the tiny white blooms clinging to my face. "No one told me I wasn't allowed. I didn't do anything wrong."

Edward stood between us in a guarding stance with his legs braced apart and his arms spread as if to hold Luke back. "Pa's just not used to having a woman around, Abby," he said in a softened voice. "He's just used to cuffing us boys around. I know he's sorry. Ain't that right, Pa?" He turned his head, glancing over his shoulder to Luke, urging him to reply.

"I ain't saying I'm sorry to no strip of a girl. She has to learn just like the rest of you did that I'm the boss around here. Now it's time supper was started. I'll be in the kitchen in an hour and I'll expect to be fed proper. Do you hear me, Abby? Answer me, girl."

Gazing up at the hard man who was my husband, I wondered how he could hurt me so badly on purpose. I knew right then I could never care for such a heartless being no matter how much I tried.

"Yes - yes, I'll start supper right away," I answered in a beaten voice. I dropped my bouquet to the ground. "My flowers are all broken."

"Them ain't flowers, they're just weeds." Luke turned on his heel and strode silently away.

"Don't feel too hard toward him, Abby," Edward said as

The Chosen Child   *Joan Hall*

he lifted me to my feet. "He's been worried lately. Things have been going on."

"What kind of things?"

"It shouldn't concern you," Edward hushed my question. "You would only worry and that wouldn't help matters a bit. Besides, you have enough on your mind with your Mama being so sick." He reached out and gently wiped a stray tear from my flushed cheek and a stray white blossom. "Poor little thing, you deserve better than this. I know it won't be easy living with Pa. He's fine as long as you don't cross him."

"But I didn't do anything wrong," I cried, the storm of rebellion building inside me.

"I know, I know," Edward soothed. "But Pa expected you to be here when he got back from town. If you were planning to not be here, you should have told him."

"I didn't plan it, it just happened."

"Well, look at it this way. Pa might have figured you had left him for good and gone back to your family, or you might have wandered from the house and got bitten by a snake or - or a wild cat could have gotten you or -or - anything."

I smiled at Edward through my pain. A wild cat hadn't been seen in these parts for years. I knew he was being the peacemaker. After his words, I did feel a little more accepting.

The Chosen Child   *Joan Hall*

Perhaps I should have left a note.

At my slight smile, Edward seemed to relax. He placed his arm around my waist and urged me toward the house. "Come on; let's put some ointment on your shoulder. The stuff always helped me." We stepped over my discarded flowers.

Perched on the edge of a chair, I loosened the neckline of my dress, careful to expose only my injured shoulder. Edward gave a low whistle. "You have a nasty gash here." He touched his salved finger to the torn skin, and I winced. "He used the end of the belt with the buckle," Edward growled. "Damn him." The rage in his voice shocked me. He had always seemed so mild mannered. I hadn't thought him capable of such strong emotion.

He continued to minister to my bruised flesh, tracing the stinging line the belt had made across the nape of my neck and shoulder. His touch felt light as he applied the cool dressing. "Pa went too far this time. He just went too far."

Chill bumps pricked my arms, and I hurriedly spoke to calm him. I couldn't bear to be the cause of more trouble, especially for dear Edward. "I'm fine, really I am. I tried to keep the pain out of my voice. It hardly hurts at all now. The salve really helped." Edward's mouth remained clenched and his brows drew together in an unrelenting scowl.

"I'm sure Luke didn't mean to injure me so badly. It

The Chosen Child   *Joan Hall*

was an accident, and he won't do it again, you'll see. I'll keep
my place from now on." Edward's face relaxed, but he didn't
speak again, and his hands trembled as he replaced the cap on
the tin of medication.

Supper that evening was eaten in silence. Luke
shoveled his food as if nothing had happened. Doyle sat staring
into space, seeming to be lost in his thoughts and Edward
pushed his food around on his plate in a pretense of eating. The
food I had hurriedly prepared seemed tasteless to me, but I
forced it down my unwilling throat.

We had just pushed away from the table when the racing
clatter of a horse's hooves shattered the evening stillness. I
raced to the window. Papa was storming up the lane astride
Homer. His hand gripped the bridle reins so tightly that the
animal's eyes bulged and his mouth fell agape. Papa rode
without his hat, so his hair blew back away from his ashen face.

Oh, his face. I moaned and fought against the wave of
nausea that threatened my consciousness. Everything slowed in
motion. With numbed eyes, I watched as my father lifted his
leg and dropped from his horse. The action seemed to take
forever, yet happened all too quickly. I wanted desperately to
stop him, to keep him from entering the house, keep him from
speaking. If I closed my mind, I wouldn't have to accept what
he had to say.

The Chosen Child   *Joan Hall*

The door burst open, thrown with such force that a framed picture jarred from the wall and crashed to the floor. For a long moment, no one spoke. Papa stood in the fading light, his face an angry troubled mask of his usual self. I broke the silence with a barely audible whisper. "Papa."

My father stood with his hands clasped to his chest as if he suffered a terrible pain inside. Finally, his voice boiled from troubled depths. "She's gone, my Molly's gone."

An animal like cry erupted from me. I didn't recognize my own voice. It couldn't be true. My mother could not be dead - gone forever. The thought of never seeing her smiling face or hearing her voice again was more than I could stand. She couldn't die without me by her side. She couldn't leave without saying goodbye.

Luke raised his hand toward Papa and opened his mouth to speak, but my father cut him off. "You lied to me," he grated, his voice reeking with disgust. "You said God told you to make her well. You had a vision, you said." Papa advanced closer and Luke took a step backwards. "You just wanted to get your dirty hands on Abby, my little girl." The grimace on his face betold his pain. "What a fool I was. I bet you laughed at me, didn't you?" His words challenged Luke, daring him to agree. "I kept Molly in that hospital with your money cause I thought they could make her well. She died over there with no

The Chosen Child   *Joan Hall*

family around." Papa's last words were a scream of anguish and angry tears streamed down his face. "She should have been home with me."

"I really thought they could heal Molly, Ezra - I really did," Luke stuttered, his face bleached of its usual reddish tone.

"I took your money, your rotten money, in exchange for my innocent daughter. I should have known better, but Molly needed treatment so bad. How could you have said you were doing God's will? How can you live with yourself?"

His tormented eyes beckoned, and I rushed into his outstretched arms. He clutched me to him as great sobs racked his body. My tears were silent, streaming from my eyes to drop on his worn shirt until a wide circle of fabric grew saturated and clung to his chest. After long moments, Papa seemed calmer and I was able to speak.

"What happened to Mama?"

"She took a real bad coughing spell and hemorrhaged." His voice broke and he wiped at his eyes before continuing. "The doctor said he just couldn't stop the bleeding."

Papa dropped his head down on my shoulder and I grimaced sharply, jerking my wounded skin away from the pressure. Stiffening in my arms, he lifted his head. While searching my eyes with his, he tugged at the collar of my dress. "What's wrong with your shoulder?" he asked, concern breaking

The Chosen Child   *Joan Hall*

through his grief.

I lifted my hand to clutch the garment together in protest, but Papa was insistent. Lowering the neckline of my dress just enough to view the raw gash marring my skin, Papa growled, and turned to face Luke. "You animal, you vile, loathsome animal. You beat my daughter." Luke raised his arms to ward off the blows that were sure to come.

"It's not like it seems, Ezra," Luke sputtered, waving his arms in the air. "I can explain."

Could Papa recognize the guilt in Luke's face? Nudging me aside, he tore at Luke. "I'll kill you, Luke Johnson," Papa swore, gnashing his teeth. The veins in his forehead swelled. "You don't deserve to live. I'll tear you limb from limb." My father swung wildly, his anger making him clumsy.

I clutched at the back of his shirt. "No. Papa, no."

Edward jumped between the two men. "Calm down, Ezra," he shouted. "Don't do something you'll be sorry for later."

"I won't be sorry," Papa grunted as he strained to reach around the boy to grab at Luke's throat.

"Papa, listen, I did it, - I did it," I screamed, but he seemed beyond hearing. Desperately, I searched my mind for a lie, a believable story. "I - I fell out of bed and hit the railing." Crossing my fingers behind my back, I cried, "I swear Papa, I swear."

I must have gotten through to him, for he uncurled his fists. Groping in his pocket, he pulled out a wad of crumpled bills. In a last burst of anger, he threw them at Luke's face. "Here, take your filthy money, I don't need it now." The bills fluttered to the floor like fallen leaves.

"No, Papa." Dropping to my knees, I grasped at the money. Doyle, who was standing by with an amused grin on his face, made a move to stoop also but was blocked by Edward. Clutching the money to my chest, I gazed up at my father. Struggling to subdue the terror in my voice, I said, "This money is for Mama."

"But Abby . . ." he began.

"I said this is Mama's money." Raising my voice, I defied my father. "It will buy her a beautiful coffin with a satin lining and a satin pillow on which to lay her head, and she will have a beautiful lace dress." I felt as if I were in a trance as I visualized Mama lying still and unmoving, her lovely face void of pain. Tears rolled anew down my cheeks. "She must have a pink dress, her favorite color. And flowers, she will have roses, red ones, pink ones and white ones. Mama loved flowers; she will have a church full of flowers."

Folding the bills, I slowly tucked them back into Papa's shirt pocket. He placed his hand over mine just above where his

The Chosen Child   *Joan Hall*

heart thudded. "Yes, daughter, she loved flowers." Papa turned and shuffled toward the door, his shoulders stooped like a man broken in body and spirit.

"Abby, I - I really am sorry." Luke's voice came out gravelly, almost soft. I could say nothing in return. All I could do was act, so I began to wash the dishes. A being didn't have to feel to work, didn't even have to think. Numbness enveloped me, drawing all my emotion into a solid box inside my chest. A lid closed tightly on the case, and then I mentally locked it and threw away the key. I didn't watch to see where the key landed because I never wanted it retrieved, just lost forever, to be rusted with time. No one would ever be able to reach inside that hidden place and expose my feelings again, no one.

Chapter Ten

Mama lay in state for one night in the house where she lived and loved. It helped to have her back in the place where she belonged, away from the cold, stark, lonely hospital. Before the neighbors arrived, all the children were allowed to say their good-byes in their own words and in their own ways.

Lucy sat quietly in her time, occasionally wiping away tears. "I'm just thinking of all the good times."

George and Josh were more vocal. George promised Mama he would be good and that he would help Papa. Josh told her of what he was going to be when he grew up and how

The Chosen Child   *Joan Hall*

much he would miss her.

When it was Paul's time, I went in search of my youngest brother. I found him at the dinner table struggling with a pencil and paper. "Abby, how do you spell love?" he asked, staring up at me with hurting eyes.

I walked over and put my arms around his small shoulders and dropped my cheek down against his. "What are you doing?"

"I'm writing Mama a letter."

"A letter?" I inquired, a bit puzzled by the means his young mind had chosen to communicate with our mother.

"Yes, a letter that she can keep with her and read anytime she wants. When she gets lonely or homesick, she can read my letter and know I love her."

"That's a wonderful idea," I told him, fighting the lump that threatened my throat.

"I know Heaven is a nice place and Mama will be happy there, but she'll miss us," he added.

"When you're finished, I'll fold the letter and we'll slip it in her hand," I whispered, giving him a big hug. Paul gave me a toothless grin.

After he printed his name, we carefully folded the paper into a small square. I lifted him up and helped him gently tuck the letter under the palm of Mama's hand.

The Chosen Child   *Joan Hall*

Finally it was my turn to be with Mama. I didn't know where to begin. But after a few minutes, words came of their own volition. "Mama, you look beautiful in your lace dress. I hope you like the roses." I hesitated and drew a long breath and allowed tears to flow. "I tried really hard to help you. Marrying Luke was the only way I knew. I'm sorry it didn't work, sorry we were too late." My voice broke on a sob, as I whispered, "Good-bye, Mama, I love you."

Papa stayed by Mama's side all the night. Many times I heard him mumbling and crying. Everyone we knew came by to show their respect and at least twenty friends remained throughout the night, giving words of comfort to Papa.

All too soon, daylight came and it was time to put Mama away. The church house had been the scene of many funerals. Death was not a stranger in our lives. In fact, it was only a month earlier that David and Mattie Stark's newborn son had been laid to rest. I tried to remember what had taken his young life. Mama had said something about him being a blue baby. Mattie had cried something terrible. Sadness swelled in my heart at the funeral but this service was different, now it was one of my own. My mother, my dear sweet Mama who was only thirty-four years old would be laid to rest. Sheer unrelenting pain coursed through me, a hurt so deep it went beyond my body and mind, wrenching my very soul. I never

The Chosen Child   *Joan Hall*

knew such pain existed.

Just once, I felt I might pass out. It would have been a relief to sink into oblivion, but Luke caught me and slapped me gently on the face.

The funeral was a solemn ritual of sermon and song. Papa sat like us children in hushed grief, the shock of our loss too great and too deep for immediate release. It was only at the end of the service when Preacher Allison closed the casket lid on Mama that he broke down, flinging himself to his knees at the altar, clutching at the coffin.

"No - no, don't take my Molly away - please. You can't take her, I won't let her go." Neighbors raced to his side and lifted his resisting body as Preacher Allison tugged his grasping hands away. They carried him from the church and still he cried out.

Finally Mama was laid to rest. Around her grave a profusion of color radiated. Roses of every hue adorned her resting place.

"I've never seen such beautiful flowers," Mrs. Warden said, wonder in her eyes.

"Molly looked lovely in her lace dress," Mrs. Suttles whispered to me.

It was strange to find comfort in such talk, but I did. To give this last gift to my mother made me happy. It had been

The Chosen Child   *Joan Hall*

well worth my own suffering.

As customary, after the service, family and friends accompanied us home. Gertrude, Papa's sister, took over at the stove and soon the aroma of frying chicken and apple pie filled the house. Becky toddled behind the woman as she rushed about the kitchen.

Finally, Aunt Gertie stooped and picked up the child and gave her a motherly hug. "Come to Aunt Gertie, baby," she said, plopping Becky astride one ample hip then easily continued with her duties.

I studied my family. The boys were already sampling Aunt Gertie's homemade dumplings. Grief held no bounds on their young appetites. The resilience of their youth would heal the pain of loss. I decided they would be fine with time. That meant three less to worry about. Dark circles under Lucy's eyes revealed the extent of her grief, but she seemed to find solace with her young friend Amos Suttles. Becky was just a baby and would soon forget. That left Papa. He moved about the guests taking comfort in each outstretched hand but his face held a strange vacant appearance. He seemed calmer now. The emotion he expelled at the church evidently left him drained and exhausted.

Luke stood apart from everyone. Occasionally, he would give Papa an uneasy glance. Finally he pulled me aside and whispered in my ear, "You stay here with your family, they need you now. I'll come back before dark to fetch you home."

"All right, Luke," I answered meekly, thankful he was allowing me this time. "I'll be ready." Luke hesitated, twisting his Sunday hat in his hands. "I said I would be ready and I meant it. We made a bargain. I'll be going home with you like I'm supposed to." Luke nodded his head and left.

Late in the evening, the last neighbor left. Aunt Gertie had tucked the older children in bed and crooned to Becky who still fretted and whimpered. Papa sat in his rocking chair restlessly urging it back and forth. I dropped to the floor beside him and lay my head on his knee. He ceased his restless movement. He spoke softly as he smoothed my tangled hair. "My Molly's in a better place, ain't she, Abby?"

"Yes, Papa, she's in a beautiful place where there's no pain or suffering. We're supposed to be happy for her, Papa."

"I just miss her so, Abby. I don't know if I can make it without her. I keep thinking about how we were just kids when we got married. She was the prettiest little thing you ever laid eyes on, not more than a hundred pounds soaking wet." He laughed softly and closed his eyes to better view the scene he was imagining. "She wanted kids right away even though she was nothing more than a kid herself, cause she loved babies. When you came along, she was the happiest I ever seen but she

The Chosen Child   *Joan Hall*

was healthy then."

Papa paused and I sat quietly, knowing it was good for him to talk about Mama. In fact I enjoyed hearing about their time together before I was old enough to recollect.

"She spoiled you something awful, never allowing you to cry. She was like a little girl with a baby doll and she wanted more so we had Lucy, then George. Things started going wrong when she got pregnant with Josh. The farm wasn't doing well; that was the summer of the drought. Molly had to learn to make do with less. It was her idea to have a midwife instead of paying a doctor."

"I remember the night Josh was born," I said, caught up in the memory of that exciting night.

"You were eight years old at the time and what a little helper you were. I'm afraid we were already growing dependent on you. You seemed like a grown-up in a little girl's body."

"Yes," I whispered. I learned early that my mother needed my help. I couldn't bring myself to tell Papa how Mama's cries had frightened me that night. Holding George on my lap, I fed him his bottle and rocked him in the big rocking chair. If I urged the chair back and forth, the creaking muffled her moans. Even then I had feared losing her.

"Molly's health just seemed to settle into a decline after

The Chosen Child   *Joan Hall*

that.   Paul's birth was difficult and then too soon she had Becky." His words trailed off into silence on a long quivering breath.

"They say time heals, Papa. Just hang on and let time help you. The children need you too, think of them."

"I'll try, daughter, I'll try."

Aunt Gertie came tiptoeing from the bedroom. "Well, the younguns are all asleep. Whew, I'm plumb tuckered." She blew in relief, and wiped at the strands of gray hair that had fallen onto her forehead. "They sure are a handful. Reminds me of my own brood when they were children." She plopped herself down on the worn sofa and it sagged beneath her large frame.

"Ezra, I've been thinking maybe I should move in here with you. You know how I've been at loose ends ever since Walter passed away, bless his soul. And the boys are all grown now with families of their own." She hesitated and smoothed the flour dusted apron over her knees. "You know me; I'm just like an old mother hen, taking all the little ones under my wing. These children here - well, they need me."

A relieved smile broke over Papa's face. "That's right kind of you Gertie. I'd be more than happy to have you. You're the answer to a - prayer." On his last words, Papa's voice faded. His gaze flashed to me, then dropped to the floor.

The Chosen Child   *Joan Hall*

"Well (the Good Lord willing) that's settled. I'll need a day to set my house in order and collect my things." Purposely, she rose to her feet. "I'll be getting off to bed now, should be a busy day for me tomorrow. I saw those apples laying out yonder in the field, going to rot. We can't have that. Yeah, this place sure does need me." Aunt Gertie mumbled under her breath as she left the room.

I lifted my head at a rap on the door. "There's Luke, I have to go."

"Are you sure, Abby? You could come back home."

"Yes, Papa, I'm sure. I took the vows that made me a Johnson." But I wasn't really sure. It would have been so good to go crawl into bed beside Becky and never have to spend another night in that old house with that old man. But I struck a bargain and duty demanded that I fulfill my side. "Besides, you have Aunt Gertie now. I won't worry so much about the kids. She'll take good care of you all."

"Yeah," Papa said, obviously relieved. "I guess I'm lucky to have her." I gave him a quick hug and hurried out the door to join my husband.

It had been a week since Mama's funeral when I awakened in the middle of the night, tossing restlessly after another nightmare. Lately my dreams were incoherent sketches

The Chosen Child   *Joan Hall*

of muddy rivers and drowning victims. Often my mother would fall in the swirling churning waters. Always, I tried to save her by throwing a lifeline, but the current was too swift, sweeping her away as she clawed madly for the rope. Other times Chris was the victim. In my dreams of him, I often swam toward him, but before I could reach his location, he would disappear beneath the surface into the murky depths. I lifted myself up from the bed because it felt damp from my perspiration. A low mumbling of voices outside my window drew my attention. Finding Luke's side of the bed empty, I rose and stepped quietly over to the open window to get a breath of fresh air. Doyle and Luke sat on the porch, speaking in hushed tones.

Suddenly Doyle erupted, his voice an angry hiss. "Pa, I tell you the revenuers are on to us. The Pendleton boys saw a fellow leaving our property about a week ago. They swore he looked like a fed. They're just waiting to catch us red-handed, you wait and see."

Luke answered in a steel hard voice, "Don't go getting all riled up, son. You say the stranger was toting a gun?"

"Yeah," Doyle grunted. "A shotgun."

"Well," Luke said calmly, "next time he comes a calling, we'll be waiting for him. He'll just have a little hunting accident. Nobody will be the wiser. We'll just let him lay for the buzzards." Luke chuckled as if the thought brought him joy

The Chosen Child   *Joan Hall*

and Doyle joined in.

My head reeled and I fell back against the wall in shocked disbelief. "Revenuers," I repeated. The realization that Luke was a moonshiner struck me. No wonder he had so much money. How could I have been so stupid? Why hadn't I figured that out sooner? I clasped my hand over my mouth to keep from shrieking when another thought hit me. Chris - Chris, my prince, was the revenuer Doyle spoke of and he was going to be killed. Surely Luke could not be so cruel. Beads of perspiration popped out on my forehead as I recalled the hard tone of his voice and knew that he could. I had to warn Chris; somehow I had to find him and let him know of the danger he was in.

When the bed sagged under Luke's weight, I lay still, pretending sleep, but my heart pounded so hard I was afraid Luke might feel the vibration against the mattress. Sleep was impossible and I could only lie there staring at the ceiling and wait for morning to come.

My hands shook so badly I could hardly prepare breakfast. I kept seeing Chris lying dead in a pool of blood. When I poured steaming coffee into Luke's cup, droplets splashed out onto his hand.

"Ouch, watch what you're doing, girl. That's hotter than hell." His piercing eyes stared at me from beneath a knotted brow.

Fear tightened my chest, making my breaths come short and rapid. "I'm sorry, I - I just haven't been the same since Mama died."

Luke barked, "Well, get a hold of yourself," then his expression relaxed, almost softened. "Why don't you spend the day with your family, Abby? It's been a week now since you've seen them. Just make sure you're back by supper time," he warned.

"I'll saddle up Lady for you before we leave," Edward volunteered quickly, giving me a sympathetic glance.

"Thank you." I almost choked on the words. So many emotions boiled around inside me, rage, fear, grief, but overshadowing all else was my concern for Chris.

The hot sun shot yellow beams through the leafy crown of the hilltops when I climbed upon the mare's back. I worried, for Luke and Doyle were hanging around near the barn. Twice I had seen them standing close with their heads bent together in secretive conversation.

"Get up, Lady." I urged the horse down the lane at a trot. First I would make a hurried visit with my family and then spend the rest of the day searching for Chris.

Aunt Gertrude met me at the door with a welcoming hug, her face lighting with a wide smile. "Land sakes, child, it's

The Chosen Child   *Joan Hall*

about time you showed up. I was about ready to come calling on you, even if I had to face that no-good husband of yours."

I breathed deeply, enjoying the embrace Aunt Gertie bestowed on me. I liked the feel of her and the scent of lavender that always wafted when she moved. Glancing around the sparkling kitchen, I noted the aroma of spice oozed from around the oven door. Becky sat in a corner, happily licking on a wooden spatula with brownish blotches of apple butter clinging to her cheeks and fingers. A sudden wave of homesickness washed over me and I moaned.

"What's the matter, dear?" Aunt Gertie held me away from her and searched my face with her eyes. "Here, come sit down." She rushed over and pulled out a chair and patted it, beckoning me to sit. "I'll fix you a cool glass of milk and you tell Aunt Gertie all about what's troubling you."

How could I tell Gertie about the young man I had met in secret? Would she understand? She would just tell Papa. With a shudder, I remembered my Papa's anger toward Luke. No, I decided. All I needed to do was find Chris. He would take care of everything.

Gertie placed the tall cold glass on the table beside me. "Here, drink this." I took a long gulp as my aunt plopped herself down on a chair opposite me. "Well?" She waited expectantly, her hands resting on her knees like she was ready to take action.

The Chosen Child   *Joan Hall*

Aunt Gertie was always ready to handle the situation, whatever that might be.

"It's just good to be home," I said. "And - I - I miss my Mama so."

"Course you do," my aunt soothed, smoothing her hand over my hair. "You belong here with your Pa. Why, you're still just a kid and married to that old man." Gertie shook her head in disgust. "I declare, I could have wrung Ezra's neck when I heard about this marriage thing, but it was too late. By the time I got word of it, you had already had your wedding night, and I knew there was no use in me putting up a fight. It's just not right to go butting in after a consummation."

Attempting to hide my warm cheeks, I lifted my glass. I was not used to such language. Aunt Gertie had always been blunt in speech. "Where are Papa and the others?" I asked.

"Ezra and the boys are pitching what's left of that hay and Lucy went to take them some cold liquid."

Draining my glass, I placed it back on the table. "Well, I had best be going."

"So soon? Well, upon my honor, you just got here," Aunt Gertie declared, her eyes wide with surprise. "You haven't had a chance to see your Papa or the kids."

"I know, but I really can't stay. I have so many things to do. I just wanted to run over and say hello."

The Chosen Child   *Joan Hall*

"But - but . . ."

I rose and rushed through the doorway in spite of Aunt Gertie's objections. As I climbed onto Lady's back, I glanced over my shoulder. My aunt stared after me, scratching her head with a bewildered expression on her face.

Silently I cried, "Oh Chris, where are you?" I reached the boundary of Luke's property and paused. Should I pass on by and ride into town? Lifting my eyes to the sky, I saw it was nearing noon. I couldn't imagine Chris sitting in that stuffy little room over the general store at this time of day. If he were trying to catch Luke making illegal liquor, then he would be staking out Luke's land somewhere.

Digging my heels into the animal's sides, I said, "Come on, Lady," and urged the animal in the direction of the mountain where I had met Chris. The still would have to be near a source of water. "The pond," I declared aloud. That was why I ran into Chris there. I had innocently stumbled onto the water supply for the still. Loosening the reins, I allowed Lady to find her way. Soon we were at the base of the mountain, just opposite where I had made my climb the week before. The house and barn were completely out of sight. The mare found a path bordering a ravine that twisted up the hill. The trail had recently been used because tracks were etched into the worn earth.

Our passage through the underbrush rustled the leaves. We were too noisy so I tied the mare to a sapling away from the path and continued the climb on foot. I took care to quieten my steps and stayed as close to the trickling branch of water as possible. When I found my way blocked by a large fallen oak, I stopped. Large branches fanned out, covering the ravine. The earth had been disturbed around the banks, like a large burrowing animal had made a home beneath the fallen tree. I crept closer and peeped inside the darkened space. What I saw made my heart jump in my chest.

Inside was a furnace formed of rock and red clay. It sat on a bedrock platform above a firebox. Atop the furnace rested a large copper bin that had been hammered to a cone shape with a pipe extending from its top, down to a barrel sitting along side.

The still! I had found Luke's still. But where was Chris? Glancing around the dense undergrowth, I called to him in a loud whisper, "Chris, this is Abby, come out, please." Receiving no reply, I called louder, "I need to see you, please; it's urgent." The thick woods silenced my desperate plea. Falling back against a tree, I smiled in relief. If he wasn't there, then Luke couldn't shoot him.

Hurriedly, I retraced my steps back down the hill. As I climbed on Lady's back, I decided to take a short cut home

The Chosen Child   *Joan Hall*

around the base of the mountain. It would take too long to go back to the main road.

Thoughts swirled around inside my head, allowing me no peace of mind. No matter how I searched for an answer to my dilemma, I simply did not know what to do. I was so lost in thought, I didn't notice that Lady had ceased her gait, and stood patiently at a barbed wire fence that blocked our way. The barrier spanned the field, to stretch up the side of the mountain.

"Darn," I spewed. "We'll have to follow the fence line until we find a gate. Come on, Lady." I directed the horse away from the mountain, along the fence. After a short distance, the animal stopped and pranced nervously. I attempted to soothe her by patting her on the shoulder. "There, there, don't be alarmed. What's wrong? What's the matter?" Lifting myself up from the saddle, I strained for a better view. Something was caught in the fence several yards away. *Probably some poor animal*, I thought. For a moment I watched for signs of struggle. After detecting no movement, I decided the unfortunate critter had died, more than likely a young inexperienced deer that had tried to jump the fence.

A sudden shiver ran over my skin. "Oh God, no," I cried, springing from the horse's back.

Fear blinded me as I bounded toward the form. My scream echoed through the valley, bouncing back to taunt me again and again. I fell to my knees beside the blue jean clad body slumped over the sharp toothed fence. A shotgun lay where it had fallen beside him. "Oh, Chris, Chris," I sobbed. With numbed fingers, I gently lifted his blood soaked head and cradled it between my hands. Convulsive tremors jerked me, as I held the unrecognizable face. Again I screamed, a shriek torn from my depths.

"They killed you . . . they killed you." Helpless dry sobs racked my body, and I swayed back and forth in a dazed rhythm. I released my hold on the corpse and stared at my blood soaked hands. On the verge of hysteria, I wiped them down the front of my dress until the garment stained red with the blood of my prince.

The sound of running feet barely registered in my paralyzed brain. "Oh Lord, what happened here?" Edward's shocked face swam before my overflowing eyes. He dropped to his knees in front of me and grabbed me by the shoulders. "Abby, what happened? Is this here man dead?"

Somehow my grief spurned anger that boiled like a stoked fire inside me. "Yes, he's dead. Your Pa and Doyle killed him. I heard them plotting last night. They killed him in cold blood."

Edward's eyes held disbelief. He scoffed. "Abby, you can't be serious. Pa is a hard man but he's not a murderer. Why would he and Doyle want to kill someone?"

"Because he was a revenuer," I answered in a steely voice. A hardness formed inside me, life was just too painful for a soft heart. The only way to survive was to be hard and callused. "Your Pa is going to answer for this, Edward, I swear."

"Are you sure, Abby? This looks like an accident to me. Look at how his gun is laying." Edward pointed his finger, forcing me to look at the damming evidence. "He must have set his gun down to climb over the fence, and then it fell and went off and shot him in the face. It sure is awful, a awful accident."

"That's what it's supposed to look like, Edward. They fixed it so it would appear like an accident to the sheriff." My voice sounded strange and unnatural, with a tight, breathless affection. Edward was not convinced. I rose on wobbly legs and staggered in a daze, blinking several times to focus my gaze. With wooden determined steps, I strode in the direction of the house and Luke.

"Don't go saying or doing something you'll be sorry for," Edward called a warning after me. Even now, he bowed to his father. Well, I was not bowing in submission. I was through giving in to Luke; past caring. What could he do to me, now that I was dead inside, he couldn't hurt me anymore. I was vaguely aware of the sight I made in my blood soaked dress.

Luke's car was parked in the lane by the barn, so that was where I directed my steps. Strangely calm, I felt like the quiet before the storm. Luke stood over a wagon wheel he was repairing. He glanced up when I stepped through the doorway.

"Abby, what's the matter?" he exclaimed, color draining from his face. "Are you hurt?" He reached out a trembling hand toward me as he glanced down my stained garment. "Your dress - your dress is all covered with blood." Staggering, he lost his balance and grabbed at the side of the wagon for support.

"Yes," I cried, my body trembling with rage, "the blood of your innocent victim."

Luke's eyes narrowed in disbelief. "What are you talking about, girl? What victim? Who's been hurt?"

How could he pretend innocence? Did he think me so unaware? Suddenly, the storm inside me broke. My thinly held emotions burst like a lightning bolt and I flew at Luke, beating him on the chest with my clenched fists. "You hateful old man, you murderer, I hate you, I hate you. You killed my prince, you killed him."

Luke grabbed my wrists, bruising my flesh, and fixed his gaze in a hardened glare. "I ain't never killed nobody." His voice growled low, dripping with spite, but I didn't cower. I stood my ground and stared into his cold eyes.

The Chosen Child   *Joan Hall*

"I heard you and Doyle plot to kill Chris last night, and I just found his body." A shudder halted my speech when I envisioned the young man's lifeless shell. "You are an evil, evil man." I threw the words at him, wanting him to hurt like I was hurting. "I hate you and I will hate you with every breath I take for the rest of my life." Never had I uttered such harsh words before, but I meant every word, hating Luke with a vengeance I had never known.

Luke sagged under my wrath, stumbling a few steps backwards. "Are you sure the young man is dead?" he asked in a stunned whisper.

"Yes, he's dead," I cried in a low ragged tone, "and you and Doyle are going to pay for it, I'll see to that."

"Blast that Doyle," Luke stormed, wiping his hand across his sweaty brow. "That boy went on his own and took a life." Striding over to the open barn door, he bellowed, "Doyle, come here right this minute." Only seconds later, Doyle stood before his father with eyes flashing first to me and then to Luke. He didn't have to say a word, his deed was written all over his face.

"You idiot." Luke swung with lightning speed and Doyle crashed to the ground at his feet. Edward walked up in time to witness the blow, holding Lady's reins in his hand. He stood by in silence as Luke and Doyle battled.

The Chosen Child   *Joan Hall*

Doyle rubbed his chin and spat blood onto the ground. "Pa, I thought I did what you wanted," he whined. "You said we'd shoot him and make it look like an accident. I didn't think I would run into him so quick, but there he was today - big as life and an easy target too. I - I thought you would be proud of me. I fired his gun into the air and fixed the body so the sheriff would think he shot himself. I was real careful and hung him on the fence just like what happened to that hunter over in Lewis a couple of years ago. I figured if it happened once it could happen again." Snickering, he added as he stared up at me. "Won't nobody know any different except Abby."

Edward groaned and turned his face to the wall away from his brother. "You fool," Luke stormed. "Don't you know when your Pa is just blowing? I'd never do something that stupid. Now we'll have the feds all over us. You really did us in this time. I ought to wring your neck"

"You have to turn him in, Luke," I snapped, swinging my gaze away from the groveling son to his father. "If you won't, I will."

Luke turned his attention back to me, staring with hard probing eyes. "You called this fellow your prince. What did you mean?"

I wouldn't let my gaze waver. "I - I met him once and - and I liked him."

The Chosen Child   *Joan Hall*

Luke's voice dropped to a husky growl, "Did you lie with him, Abby?"

It was seconds before I realized what Luke was asking. But I was quick to assure him. "No, no, I never lay with him, Luke, I swear."

For an instant, Luke's face spread in relief, then his voice tightened as he asked, "Did you love the man?"

Hesitating, I wondered if I even knew what love was. For a brief instant, I recalled the sweet rush of feeling when Chris placed his lips on mine. With closed eyes, I recalled the sound of his voice and his handsome smiling face. "Yes," I breathed on a sigh. "I loved him."

Luke straightened his shoulders to their fullest height. "Well, then I'm glad he's dead. If I had known about your tryst, I would have shot him myself. I could just as easily be the guilty one instead of Doyle."

"If you won't tell the sheriff, then I will," I screamed. I whirled and grabbed Lady's reins from Edward's hand.

"Stop her, Pa," Doyle shouted.

Strong wiry arms grabbed me around the waist and dragged me backwards. "You can't stop me." I dug at the clutching hands. "I'm going to tell. I'm reporting Doyle. Let go of me."

"What are we going to do, Pa? We can't let Abby talk.

The Chosen Child   *Joan Hall*

We got to shut her up." Doyle crouched on the ground, anxiously rubbing his hands up and down his arms. His face cried desperation as he pleaded to his father.

"Let me handle this." Luke spoke in a granite hard voice. "Abby, I have no choice; I got to protect my own. Doyle may not be the brightest, but he's my son. I got nothing to lose now with one dead man on my hands."

Dread clawed at my heart, stilling me. Cautiously, I lifted my gaze to meet my husband's stare, "What are you getting at, Luke?"

"I mean, if you sacrifice my son, then I'll have to kill your Pa - an eye for an eye." His words were a weapon stabbing me in the heart.

"No, you wouldn't," I cried. My legs buckled.

"Oh - yes - I - would." Luke spoke his deadly threat in hard precise words.

"Pa, you don't mean that," Edward exclaimed, breaking his silence. He reached his hand out toward his father.

"I never meant anything more in my life," Luke growled in my ear. Edward dropped his hand and his head.

I ceased struggling as waves of chills shook me. Lifelessly, I sagged against Luke. He let go, giving my body a push away from him. I collapsed on the ground at his feet. Edward rushed to my side and laid his arm around my

The Chosen Child   *Joan Hall*

shoulders.

"Doyle, you better go into town and let the sheriff know about the accident that happened here today," Luke said. "Tell him you just happened to discover the body while you were checking the fence row. We got to carry this thing you started through to the end." Luke stepped over me and strode out of the barn with stiff purposeful strides, never giving me a backward glance.

I lay where I had fallen, for I hadn't the strength to go on. How could I have thought I could win against the likes of Luke Johnson? I should never have tried. I was no match for his wickedness.

"Come on, Abby, I'll help you to the house." Edward tugged at my shoulders, urging my limp body upward. He lifted me into his arms, for I felt unable to move. Laying my head against his chest, I heard the even thumping of his heart. "Abby," he appealed, as he carried me toward the house. "You got to learn how to live with this family. You have to keep quiet and not step on toes. If you keep quiet and stay out of the way, like I do, everything is fine. Stop challenging Pa."

His words registered in my brain, but I felt no urge to respond. Strangely, I was not really inside my body. It was just an empty sheath; my real being had hidden somewhere far away, so far away that not even I could find myself.

"Look at you," he groaned, "all covered with blood." He deposited me on my bed then began unbuttoning the front of my dress. I didn't resist when he pulled the garment over my head. "We'll have to burn this thing."

That's part of Chris, I thought as I stared at the discarded blood stained smock, *going to be tossed and burned like trash*. Still, I didn't object.

He grabbed my hands and turned them over for inspection. "I'll get a cloth." A few minutes later, Edward returned with a warm, wet rag. Taking each of my hands, he gently washed away all traces of my prince. Edward could wipe away the blood, but he could not erase Chris from my heart, nor could he cleanse away the evil deed that his brother had done, not with all the soap and water in the world.

Carefully, Edward pushed me down on the bed. The coolness of the sheets soothed my flushed cheeks, and I burrowed my head into the pillow. I didn't even care that I was only modestly covered in my petticoat.

"You'll feel better after a while," he crooned as he brushed my hair back with a trembling hand. I didn't answer. What was the use? Instead, I stared at the faded walls until my eyes burned. Edward paced the room, occasionally breathing a long sigh.

"It ain't gonna help anything for you to go making

The Chosen Child   *Joan Hall*

yourself sick. That young fellow is dead and there's nothing we can do about it now. I don't like it either. Doyle has done a lot of things he shouldn't have and this is the worst. We can't undo this deed, as bad as it is; you'll just have to accept that."

Edward's words held no meaning. Those words were for the old Abby. There was no room for feelings in my new place, this dark empty void where my troubled soul found peace. I would not leave this new world for anyone.

His pacing halted and he stood at the foot of my bed, staring at me. "Oh God, what have they done? What have I let them do to you? Abby, I'm sorry. I can't change the murder, but I'll try to set things right, I swear." Edward turned and with quiet steps left the room.

The Chosen Child   *Joan Hall*

Chapter Eleven

Through necessity, I rose from my bed. Meals still had to be cooked and chores had to be done. I did my work in stony silence, my body performing, almost without conscious thought. Luke and Doyle accepted my muteness without concern, but Edward watched me constantly with worried eyes. On the third day, when I still showed no signs of my normal self, Edward exploded. I had numbly cleared the table after the evening meal.

"Pa, you just got to do something about Abby. Look at her, she's sick. We ought to have a doctor check her. She's getting thin too. I - I'm worried about her, Pa."

Luke's gaze scoured over me. "Ah, she's just pine-in' away over her lover. Sooner or later she'll come out of it and realize no amount of grieving will bring that young fellow back; he's gone for good and good riddance too. He got what he deserved for fooling around with a married woman."

Something stirred deep within me. I could almost recall the sweet sensation I felt when Chris kissed me, almost, but not quite. Even his memory was shrouded in a thick gray fog.

I had just closed the bedroom door to lie down when a loud rap sounded on the front door. Who would come calling at Luke Johnson's I wondered. It really didn't matter.

The rapping came again, only louder, the sound seeping through the thin wall into my room. "Who in tarnation?" Luke thundered as he stomped across the floor and jerked open the portal.

"Evening, Luke," Aunt Gertie said. My heart roused at the familiar voice, but then settled back to its steady rhythm. "I came to see my niece, Abby. I've been worried about her. It's been days since we talked and the last time I saw her, she just wasn't herself." Aunt Gertie's voice grew stronger. She had evidently pushed her way into the living room. "Where is she?"

"She's resting," Luke answered.

"At this time of day?" Gertie's voice held disbelief.

The Chosen Child   *Joan Hall*

"The only way a girl that age would be in the bed now, is if she was sick." Gertie raised her voice and called to me, so loudly, she would surely be heard through the closed bedroom door. "Abby, it's your Aunt Gertie, honey. I came calling to see about you."

"I said she was resting," Luke roared in his most threatening manner.

"Then it won't hurt if I just open the door and take a peek at her, will it?" Aunt Gertie said, rapping on my door. When I didn't respond, she opened the door and stuck her head inside the darkened room. Not satisfied with seeing me stretched out on the bed, she entered the room and tiptoed over to stand beside my bed.

Aunt Gertie moaned when her gaze probed my blank, staring eyes. Throwing her hand up, she covered her shocked whisper, "Holy Jesus, what's happened to you, child?" She rushed over and raised the blinds on the windows and allowed the late sun to brighten the room. "Oh you poor baby," she cried, when she noticed the thinness of my body and the dark shadows around my eyes. "You're wasting away." She ran her fingers down my slim arms, and then placed her hand under my chin to turn my face for her inspection. "Oh, Abby," she soothed as she pulled my limp form upright in bed and held me against her breast. "What's wrong, honey? Tell Aunt Gertie.

The Chosen Child   *Joan Hall*

Are you sick?" I managed to shake my head. "Well, something's mighty wrong. I heard about that young man shooting himself the other day on Luke's property. Is that what's upsetting you?"

I shuddered. "My prince - my prince," I murmured.

"There, there," my aunt purred, patting my shoulder. She pulled me close then rocked me back and forth as she often did Becky when the baby was fretting. Her movements kept time with the loud tic-tock of the mantel clock in the front room. "Accidents happen, sweetheart. We just have to learn to accept these things. You just can't go getting so upset."

My frozen heart almost cracked. It would be good to unload all my pent up anguish onto Aunt Gertie's strong shoulders and leave this empty place. My lips mumbled against her comforting breast. I had been mute for so many days that my mouth would not interpret the weak impulse from my brain.

"What's that, child? What did you say?" Aunt Gertie pushed me away to search my face with her sharp eyes.

"That's long enough, Gert." Luke's voice was a tight, anxious rasp. He had crept into the room and stood like a beast paused for attack, guarding his prey. "Abby needs her rest. You'd best be going now."

"This girl needs me, Luke. I think I'd better take her home with me for a spell - just till she feels better," my aunt said, smoothing my limp hair away from my face.

"No." The word burst from Luke like a shot from a rifle. Aunt Gertie flinched in alarm and I withdrew from her arms and lay back down on the bed, drawing my knees up toward my chin. "Abby belongs here now. She's my wife and don't you forget it. She ain't going nowhere with you." Luke marched across the room to tower over my aunt. He reached down and grabbed her arm and pulled her to her feet. "Come on, I'll see you to the door."

"Now wait just a gosh-darned minute," Aunt Gertie ranted uselessly.

Although she resisted, Luke's powerful arms dragged her across the room and through the bedroom doorway leaving the door open. "If you don't let Abby come home with me, I'll send Ezra after her." Luke didn't respond. I watched as he shoved Aunt Gertie out the front door, slamming it behind her. "You'll be sorry for this, you old buzzard." Aunt Gertie yelled. "I'm going to go home and tell Ezra right now that his girl is in need, so you just be prepared to give her up! You hear?

Don't you worry none, Abby, your Pa will be coming to get you." Aunt Gertie yelled at the top of her voice. She waited on the porch and when she got no answer, stormed off and climbed in her wagon. The leather reins slapped against the horse's rump, as she urged him off at a gallop.

"Boys," Luke growled. "I want you to be clearing things up around here. Finish that run you started. I think we ought to move down to Tennessee for a spell. I knew that little piece of property I bought down there would come in handy someday. We can hide out in those mountains till doomsday and they never will find us."

"Pa, are you crazy?" Edward said. "You mean to pull up stakes - just like that and move to Tennessee?"

"That's exactly what I mean," Luke muttered. "Nobody will know where to look for us." He jerked open the top drawer of the bureau that sat in the corner of the living room. "We can be out of here in a few days." They were unmindful of my staring gaze through the doorway from the bedroom.

"What's the matter, Pa? Are you afraid of little Ezra Potter? Are you going to turn tail and run?" Doyle snickered as he lounged against the wall. Luke turned as he lifted something from the drawer. Doyle's face paled and he stammered, "Now, look Pa, I was just kidding."

"This whole dang mess is your fault, Doyle. The feds are doing an inquiry into that young man's death. The sheriff told me he had to make a statement." I watched from my bed as he stroked his fingers over the shiny black steel of the thirty-eight pistol he clutched in his hand. Giving a scathing laugh, he said, "But don't worry, this ain't for you."

The Chosen Child   *Joan Hall*

"Pa, what in heaven's name are you going to do with that thing?" Edward stood in the center of the room, shaking, his arms clutched about himself.

"I ain't about to let Ezra come and take my wife. I'm going to meet him down the road and the two of us is gonna have it out, once and for all." Luke's voice grated like steel on steel.

"Pa, ain't there been enough killing," Edward pleaded. "Leave Ezra alone, he'll cool down. We'll just tell him that Abby has the flu or the summer complaint. He's never been a violent man."

"All the more reason to fear him," Luke declared. "It's the quiet folk like Ezra you have to be prepared for. He'll let his anger seethe till he blows. Well, I'm going to stop him before he gets to that point. He's not going to get out of my control."

"Maybe - Maybe Abby ought to go home - just for a little while - till she gets to feeling better. She is doing poorly. Please, Pa." Edward said.

"Ain't you forgetting something, son? Abby knows about Doyle killing that young man. The first thing she's going to do is tell her Papa about it. We're trapped, Edward. I ain't got no choice. It's Ezra or me. This thing is just getting plumb out of hand." Luke flipped open the round cylinder of the gun and slid bullets into the dark holes. Luke's jerky motions reminded me of a cornered animal. I watched in silence, noting every movement, but my heart remained a cold lump in my chest.

"Pa, let me go in your place," Edward begged, stepping between Luke and the door. With his hand outstretched, he grabbed at the gun but Luke jerked it away. "I can reason with Ezra. He has always been a level headed man. There's no sense in you toting a gun. Pa." Edward lunged, grabbing his father around the chest in a last desperate attempt to stop his father. "Ezra just lost his wife and he still has five kids to raise. If you go and kill him, what's going to happen to them poor younguns with no Ma or Pa about?"

Luke hesitated for an instant, and then thrust out his arm, throwing Edward aside. "This is self defense, son. I'm just protecting myself. The sheriff will see just cause." His mouth drew down at the corners and he pushed at his son's chest, growling, "You always were too soft-hearted, son. You're too much like your mother."

"Doyle, Doyle, you stop him," Edward appealed to his brother who had been strangely quiet. He grabbed at Doyle's shirt sleeve. "We can't let him go and kill Ezra. It just ain't right. We got to stop him. Ezra's a good man."

"Leave Pa alone, Edward, you know there ain't no stopping him when he's got his mind set on something." Doyle

The Chosen Child   *Joan Hall*

turned his back on Edward, pulling free of his grasp, away from the pleading eyes. "Pa started this whole thing by taking Abby as his wife against her will. I guess he'll have to be the one to finish it."

I watched the happenings in the next room without emotion. They were bad actors on a stage, quoting lines of fiction. No stirring of rage or fear gripped me. Not even the thought of my unsuspecting father being outmatched by Luke and his firearm could rouse me from my stupor.

Luke retrieved his hat and tugged it down over his eyes before opening the front door. "I ain't looking forward to this chore and I'm not going to do anything I don't have to. It's all up to Ezra but he's not taking Abby from me. You both heard him threaten me after Molly died. He's just been waiting for a good excuse."

Within the doorway, Luke's figure stood dark and foreboding, outlined by the late rays of sunshine streaming around him. His huge shadow stretched over the length of the room, seeming much bigger than life, dwarfing his sons. For a long moment, he stood in silence, staring at his boys, his jaw set in a tightened grimace. With the slam of the door, he was gone.

"I got things to do," Doyle muttered as he turned and exited toward the back door leaving Edward standing alone. Footsteps echoed through the house as Edward paced back and forth, muttering under his breath, only raising his voice with a distinguishable, "Damn." When his fist slammed against the wall, the force jarred me to some awareness.

"Edward, what's wrong?" I finally found my voice and it was weak and scratchy, sounding unnatural to my ears.

Edward's head jerked upward. I stood in the doorway of my bedroom. "Nothing for you to worry about," he answered.

But even in my state, I recognized the desperation that twisted his face. "Is my Aunt Gertie gone?"

"Yeah, she went back home, Abby."

"Where's Doyle?" I asked woodenly.

"I don't know - maybe he's out in the barn. Excuse me, Abby," Edward mumbled as he brushed past me and left the house.

The house seemed awfully quiet. My mind was used to quietness lately. No thoughts or fears raced around in the empty space to inspire me to action. I functioned, but only from habit. Silently I walked around the room; for more than an hour I plumped pillows and put things in their rightful places. The gold framed mirror hanging on the wall hung askew. No matter how many times I straightened the thing it always leaned to one side.

A blank haunted face stared back at me from the cracked glass. I didn't recognize the thin frail girl whose dress hung on

The Chosen Child   *Joan Hall*

a bony frame. Slowly, I raised my hand and traced the hollows in the cheeks. Was that strange vacant reflection in the mirror really me? No light shone in the clouded gaze. It was as if life itself had slipped out of the figure and left a dead shell of a person. For a long moment I stared then something broke inside me.

I don't want to be dead, I want to live. The plea erupted somewhere deep within my young heart. I could not give up the fight this easily. Pain was a part of life, as was joy, from birth to death, and must be endured. Pain might even give me strength if I could learn to harness it.

Raw terror seized me as I realized what had almost happened to me. I had run from pain - run from the struggle with life and my battle with Luke's control, almost never to return. "Oh. Aunt Gertie," I moaned, recalling the comforting sensation of being held against her soft bosom. My aunt was a strong woman, whom I had always admired, often thought I took after her, considered myself to be of the same strong character. I would have to fight to regain the confidence that had hidden along with my emotions.

Tears swelled inside me and erupted to rain down my cheeks. The tears acted as a release, washing away pent up anguish. I cried for myself, the loss of my mother, whom I loved more than life, and Chris, the young prince who touched my life so briefly and gave me a glimpse of true happiness.

"Damn you, Luke Johnson," I shrieked. He had destroyed everything good about my life and I had almost let him destroy me as well. And now he was waiting to confront Papa with a gun. Helplessness again caught hold of me and I almost receded. With a glance at the clock I knew the situation was now beyond my control. It was too late for me to intervene. The two men would have already met down the road. I would have to rely on Papa's good sense and on God to see him through.

Red hot anger seized me. I rushed across the room and grabbed the cast iron rooster doorstop that held the heavy oak door wide. It took all my strength to throw the object. The offending mirror crashed to the floor, shattering into small fragments. With a smile, I thought, *it's too bad I wasn't aiming at Luke's head.*

I lay for hours anticipating Luke's return from the confrontation with Papa. Even though my father would have been angry, he was a kind man, and basically had a wit about him, so I knew he would act responsibly. Luke was a cautious man also, I assured myself. Look how he had responded to Doyle's actions, charging him with stupid behavior for shooting Chris, yet I tossed with worry. Hours ticked slowly by. My husband should have been back. Finally, after the clock struck

The Chosen Child   *Joan Hall*

twelve, my exhausted mind fell into deep sleep in spite of my resolve to keep my eyes open.

A loud rapping at the front door startled me to wakefulness. Daylight peeked around the drawn shade at the lace covered window. Luke's pillow lay round and plump, evidence that he had not come to bed last night. *It must be eight o'clock*, I thought, as I jerked up in bed.

"Hold on, hold on, I'm coming." Doyle's loud reply rang through the house as the knocking sounded again.

A sense of dread consumed me. Something was terribly wrong. I rose with my heart pounding and tiptoed over to the door. I placed my ear against it to better hear. "Sheriff Nolan, what are you doing way out here so early in the morning?" Doyle asked through an exaggerated yawn.

I dropped to my knees before the generous sized keyhole in the bedroom door and peeked through. Doyle stood at the entry before the sheriff, stretching out his hand in greeting. His shirt was only half buttoned and his feet were bare.

"Morning, Sheriff," Edward said. He had followed his brother into the room. As usual Edward appeared neatly dressed and groomed for the day. "Would you like a cup of hot coffee? I made it myself."

"No, boys." Sheriff Nolan cleared his throat and pulled his hat from his head. He stood twisting it in his hands. "This ain't no social call. I got some bad news to tell you." The sheriff glanced around the room. "Where's Abby?" he asked.

"She's still sleeping," Edward said, his voice growing tight. "What's up, Sheriff?"

"I'm glad Abby's not going to hear this. I don't relish telling that girl about all this, I'll leave that up to you fellows."

Oh, no, no, no, not my Papa, I can't lose my Papa too.

"Tell her what?" Doyle demanded. "Sheriff, I think you'd better level with us."

"Well, I'm sorry, boys, but Luke is dead. Ezra came to me about ten last night. He was real upset - shaking like a leaf. He reported finding Luke's body lying beside the road - said he just found him there; said he was coming to get Abby and take her home where she belonged."

"No, no, it can't be." Edward's cry of denial faded as I fell against the door in shock. My father was safe; instead, it was Luke who had been slain. Never again would I have to bear his touch. Shame washed over me and I cringed at my selfish sense of relief.

"Pa was meeting Ezra and they were going to fight," Doyle volunteered. His voice rose to a high excited state.

"I reckon I'll have to arrest Ezra for the killing," Sheriff Nolan said reluctantly.

"No, Papa would never do such a thing." I clasped my

hand over my mouth, afraid my words might be heard in the next room. Papa was easy to anger but underneath he was like a puppy. In all of my sixteen years I had never known him to strike a hard blow to another being; even when I or the boys misbehaved we had never gotten more than a light smack from him. Pressing my face to the door again, I decided I must hear every word spoken and see every move.

"Sheriff, how did Pa die and what makes you think Ezra did it?" Edward wrung his hands and his face appeared distraught.

"Your Pa took a blow to the head from a rock. It was lying there on the ground next to him, all covered with blood. Besides I found some evidence. This here's Ezra's handkerchief and it was laying beneath Luke's body." The sheriff pulled a crumpled stained piece of cloth from his shirt pocket. "See here, it's got the initials EP stitched on it. Many's the day I saw Ezra use it." He folded the fabric and tucked it away.

"But anybody could have struck Pa down. You know he always carried a pocket full of money; maybe he was robbed," Edward volunteered.

"No, he still had his billfold in his pocket where it belonged. No sir, robbery wasn't the motive behind this killing, something a little more complicated, I'm afraid."

In silence, Doyle witnessed the exchange between his

brother and the sheriff. His face held a rock hard expression except for a nervous twitch in his jaw.

"But to think that Ezra could do this is just crazy. He's a gentle soul," Edward said.

"Yeah, but even a gentle man can be pushed too far. Everybody in the county knows about this deal he and Luke cooked up."

"But how . . ." Edward began.

Sheriff Nolan took off his hat and wiped the sweat from his forehead on the sleeve of his shirt, then placed the worn, stained Stetson back on his head before speaking.

"The evening that Molly passed away, Ezra was mighty upset and rightfully so. He had to come into town to pick out Molly's coffin you know." Nolan shifted uncomfortably and lowered his gaze to his hands. "A few drinks made it easier I'm sure. Everybody needs a crutch every now and then."

The sheriff took the time to draw a long breath then continued. "Well according to Ellis, he pulled out a wad of bills to pay for the funeral and all the trimmings he ordered, then he wiped his hands down the front of his clothes and burst out crying - said it was dirty money, money that Luke gave him for Abby - said that Luke didn't deserve to live. Well, it didn't take long for that busy-body wife of Ellis's to tattle such a juicy tale. Now everybody knows and with Luke being found dead it sure

The Chosen Child   *Joan Hall*

looks bleak for Ezra.

When he came and reported finding Luke's body lying beside the road, he said he was coming to get Abby and take her home where she belonged. Man, what a mess," the sheriff muttered, "I ain't seen nothing like this since John Cooke stole Walter Jordan's wife. Everybody agreed John got what was coming to him. I just don't know how folks are going to feel about this situation.

Well boys, I better go. I sure am sorry about Luke. Man I hate to arrest Ezra but I got no choice. It's just too cut and dried." Sheriff Nolan turned and marched his large frame toward his beat up station wagon.

In stunned disbelief, I fell weakly against the door, my whole body quaking. Papa could not have murdered Luke, I knew him too well. Someone else was the culprit - someone like Doyle. Tears coursed down my face. This was all my fault. If only I had been born ugly, with thick course features and dull hair, my life would not have wreaked such havoc. Biting my trembling lip, I wondered how many more lives were going to be lost due to my actions, there could be no more - no more. The slam of the front door, as the sheriff left, brought my attention back to the two brothers in the living room.

"Damn, I can't believe he's gone," Doyle grunted, his voice disbelieving. "Just a blow to the head from a rock took him. Why, I've given him some mighty hard knocks and he never went down. I always thought he was indestructible."

"Yeah, me too," Edward agreed breathlessly.

"Sit down, Edward," Doyle muttered in an unusually soft voice. "You look like you're going to pass out." I strained to hear every word the two were saying.

Edward dropped into a chair as if he hadn't the strength to continue standing. He whispered, "It's just the two of us now."

"You mean the three of us, don't you?" Dolye said, his voice growing harder and sounding very much like his father. "We still have Abby."

"But Abby will go back home now, Doyle. She's sick. Something happened to her mind. She needs to be with people who will love her and take care of her."

For a while I had forgotten about the secretive place where I had been for the last weeks. I must have been a wreck for Edward to worry so about me. He and Doyle had no knowledge of my new-found strength. I decided to keep it a secret for now. It would serve me better to let them think I was still incapacitated.

"She ain't got nobody now," Doyle said. "With Ezra in jail and her mother gone, she's our responsibility."

Could Doyle really be concerned with my well being? I

knew with his next words. "Besides, Abby is a widow now, and as Pa's wife she is due half of everything in Pa's name, and you know how Pa was, that means everything; the farm, money, everything we own will be Abby's." Doyle's voice hardened. "I tried to get Pa to make a will. He said he had plenty of time for that later." Doyle groaned. "Lord, I never thought he would die. I still can't believe he's gone. I expect to see that door thrown open any minute now and Pa come striding through. It's just not right for him to be dead." Doyle's voice dropped to a hushed questioning tone. "Do you reckon Ezra really killed Pa?"

"Yeah, I reckon he did," Edward conceded in a weak voice.

"I guess it's up to me to take over now," Doyle stated in a matter-of-fact tone. "We'll have to wait till after Pa's funeral, but then I'll sell the rest of our stash of liquor and destroy the still and all the evidence. With all them revenuers closing in, we got to have a clean place, and then we'll pull up stakes and head for Tennessee like Pa wanted us to do. We can start all over where they'll never find us - just you - and me - and Abby."

"I'm scared, Doyle." Edward sighed with a trembling voice. "Our whole world is falling apart. I just don't think I can make it with Pa gone."

"Just you leave everything to me. I can run things just

as good as Pa."

"I guess I'd better go and tell Abby what happened," Edward said reluctantly.

"No." The word burst from Doyle. "I think I'd better be the one to break the news to Abby." Doyle raised, pulled himself up to his fullest height and placed deliberate steps toward where I huddled.

I rushed quickly to the bed, stretched out and pulled the sheet up to my chin, assuming an uninterested pose just before Doyle burst through the door without bothering to knock.

"Abby," he called, an urgency in his voice. "Wake up, I got something awful to tell you."

"What is it, Doyle?" I spoke in a monotone and held my gaze in a blank stare.

"Pa's dead," he blurted. "He was killed last night - uh - somebody hit him in the head with a rock." Doyle waited for my reaction, his keen eyes centered on my face.

I stared unblinking into the features that were so much like Luke's, the same small grey eyes deep set beneath protruding brows, same narrow nose and tight thin lips. "Luke is dead?" I asked, as thought unable to comprehend. "That means another funeral, doesn't it?" I displayed no emotion. "I will wear my best dress - my wedding dress." Lifting my eyes to hold Doyle's gaze, I asked innocently, "Should I wear my

The Chosen Child   *Joan Hall*

wedding dress, Doyle?"

Doyle shifted uncomfortably. "Yes - yes, Abby, wear your wedding dress." For an instant his pale eyes probed mine. His gaze lowered, sweeping my figure partially covered by the thin sheet then he stared at the empty side of the bed. He stretched out his hand and pressed it into Luke's pillow as if testing it for comfort. My breath caught. It took all my control to keep from slapping the offending hand away from the bed.

"Me and Edward will go to town and take care of the arrangements," Doyle said. "As soon as Ellis can get Pa ready, we'll bring him back here to the house for the wake. That will probably be about seven o' clock or so tonight. We'll have the grave dug next to Ma's and lay him to rest tomorrow. Ain't no use in dragging these things out - just makes it hard on everybody. When a man is dead - he's dead. There's no use worrying about it." Doyle's voice faltered slightly on his last words and he rubbed his hand over his face. "Pa is really gone," he said and rose stiffly to his feet then stepped away from the bed.

I lay still until the hum of the car engine echoed through the house, and then I jumped to my feet. I had until maybe six o'clock - no - five o'clock, just to be safe. I knew what I had to do. I had to save my Papa. I didn't know how but I knew I had to try.

Chapter Twelve

The old station wagon sputtered and lurched the last few yards up the ruddy lane to cough to a halt in front of Papa's graying clapboard house. I hid behind the door of the smoke house that sat just to the left rear of the house. By riding the mare in a direct line across the hills, I had managed to arrive just a few minutes before the sheriff pulled up. My father sat in the porch swing, urging it silently back and forth. Becky snuggled in his lap, her eyes closed in peaceful sleep. Crouching low, I rushed over to stand pressed against the side of the house just out of sight.

The Chosen Child   *Joan Hall*

"Howdy, Sheriff," Papa said in a voice softened so as not to waken the sleeping baby. "Come on up and have a seat." Sheriff Nolan took his time climbing the three steps, and then eased his big frame into the rocking chair.

"I guess you took care of Luke, didn't you?" Papa asked, and then added as an afterthought, "Did you get to see Abby? Is she taking it well?"

Nolan leaned back in the chair and stretched his legs out in front of him. "I didn't get to see Abby, just the boys. I figured I'd let them break the news to her. Man, I'm tired," he said changing the subject. "I didn't even go to bed last night, did you?"

"Just for a spell this morning," Papa said with a thoughtful look on his face. "It's hard to go to sleep after you find a man lying dead, even a cold-hearted brute like Luke. No man deserves to die like that - without dignity." He stared down at his youngest daughter, resting in his lap.

"There ain't nothing like holding a baby in your arms, is there, Nolan?" Papa gazed off into the distant hills. "Except maybe holding your wife," he added, his voice breaking.

"No, I reckon there ain't," the sheriff agreed.

Brightening, my father said, "Becky is doing a lot better. She don't cry for her Mama now. Gertie's been a right good Nana for the kids. They're well fed and clean and mind their

The Chosen Child   *Joan Hall*

manners."

"Did I hear my name mentioned?" Aunt Gertie stuck her smiling face out from behind the screen door. She wore a blue dotted apron with the usual smudges of white flour on the bosom. "Hi, Sheriff, I thought I heard you pull up. Would you like a cup of coffee?"

"I don't care if I do, Gert. Thank you." She handed him a steaming cup. "Ezra told me about Luke. I'd like to say I'm sorry, but I can't, cause that man was evil through and through. Poor little Abby has suffered at his hand. I expect I'll go over later to help the child. She won't know how to cope with being a widow no more than she knew how to be a wife."

Sheriff Nolan grunted as if he hadn't a reply and took a sip of his coffee. "Did you figure out what happened to Luke?" Gertie asked as she sat down in the only other chair. He turned his gaze upon my father. "Ezra said his head was all bloody."

Shifting uncomfortably in his chair, Nolan said, "Yeah, I think I figured out what happened. Ezra, how did you get those smudges of blood all over your shirt?"

"Why - why - I rolled Luke over to see how bad he was hurt. I wanted to see if he was still alive - so I could help him." Papa stumbled over his words and leaned forward in the swing. Becky whimpered. "Sheriff, you don't think I killed Luke? I was mad at him - hell, I'll admit I hated the man, but I didn't want to see him dead. I just wanted my daughter back, that's all."

"Ezra, the evidence is strong; I found your handkerchief under Luke's body. Now, how did it get there?"

"Well, I was going to stop the bleeding but I saw it was too late," Papa said with a stunned look on his face. "I guess I rolled Luke back over. I don't remember really - I was in shock."

"You rolled a dead man back over onto his face?" The sheriff asked. "That just don't sound right, Ezra and you know it."

"But it's the truth, Sheriff."

Aunt Gertie had been sitting in silence. Finally, she couldn't contain her anger any longer and jumped to her feet. "Sheriff, are you accusing Ezra of murder?"

Nolan's round face reddened and he lowered his gaze. "Who else could have wanted him dead? Everybody knows how Luke got Abby for a wife, and Doyle will testify that Luke was going to meet Ezra for a showdown - and with blood all over Ezra and the handkerchief. It's a mighty tight case for murder, if you ask me."

"It looks suspicious, Sheriff, but I swear by all that's holy I didn't kill Luke. I was going to slug it out with him if I had to, but all I wanted was to get Abby out of his clutches."

The Chosen Child   *Joan Hall*

"Ezra, you're a small man and Luke stood at least six feet. We all know you'd be no match for him in a fair fight. You would have been foolish to even try. So I figure you had to use the rock in self defense. It was self defense - wasn't it, Ezra?" Nolan prodded him to agree. "It will be a lot easier for you if you say you had to protect yourself."

"Now don't go trying to put words in my mouth. I ain't going to confess to something I didn't do." Papa set his chin in a stubborn pose and turned his head away to signal the subject was closed.

"Well, Ezra, you give me no choice. I hate to do this but - but I got to take you in."

Aunt Gertie caught her breath. She rose from her chair and stomped over to stand in front of Sheriff Nolan. "You can't do this. What about the children; they've already lost their mother, and now you want to put their father in jail." She reached out and grabbed the coffee mug from the startled man's hand, sloshing the last of the brown stuff on his lap. "If I had known what you were up to I wouldn't have been so neighborly."

Sheriff Nolan's jaw fell in shocked reaction to my aunt's sharp tongue. Quickly, he rose from his chair and stepped around her straight, angry figure and spoke in a rush. "Ezra, I got a lot of paperwork to do. You get yourself a change of clothes and come along peaceful like."

"Give me a few minutes to put Becky to bed and tell the other children," my father mumbled in a resigned voice.

"Okay, but don't dally too long, I'm a tired man."

Moments later, the squalls of crying children burst through the screen door. "See what you've done," my aunt grated through clenched teeth. "You've gone and upset all those kids. Now I'll have a heck of a time getting them hushed."

As he stepped from the house, Papa carried a worn satchel. He said, "Don't worry, Gert, we'll get this thing straightened out. Keep the kids in line, I'll be back soon." For a moment he hesitated, then lifted his shoulders to stand a little taller. "At least I know that my Abby is safe now."

After watching the car sputter down the lane, Aunt Gertie dropped into a chair and let her head fall into her hands. Lost in despair, she didn't notice my figure rushing toward her. Only when the slight weight of my hand touched her shoulder did she stir. "Abby - Abby," she cried, jumping to her feet and giving me a big hug.

"Aunt Gertie," I squealed as my aunt clutched me close.

"Oh child, you're home. You won't have to go back to that awful Johnson house again." Holding me back away from her, she eyed me carefully. "You're so thin." Noting the anguish in my eyes, Aunt Gertie whispered, "You know about

The Chosen Child   *Joan Hall*

Ezra, don't you?"

"Yes, I overheard the sheriff this morning when he brought the news about Luke. Oh Aunt Gertie, Papa couldn't have killed Luke."

"I know, child, but somebody did and made it look bad for Ezra."

With a catch in my voice, I gushed, "Awful things have been happening. I have to tell you about them. I - I knew the young man who was killed on Luke's property. His - his name was Chris and he was awfully nice."

Aunt Gertie groaned. "Why didn't you tell me you knew him? You poor child." She smoothed back my hair in a loving fashion.

"I couldn't - I just couldn't talk about it. I couldn't even face it, Aunt Gertie. I - I slipped away, inside my head." Struggling, I tried to unload the burden that had held me prisoner for the last days. "I was in another place." Wringing my hands, I gazed into my aunt's eyes. I needed her to understand. Aunt Gertie was wise and experienced and could help me to understand what had happened.

"I don't mean a real place, just in here." I tapped the side of my head with a finger. "It was a quiet place where I could rest and not feel pain. But I really didn't want to stay there because it was so empty I got lonely."

The Chosen Child   *Joan Hall*

"Oh, baby," my aunt soothed. "I know - I know." She took my hand and pulled me down to rest in the chair Sheriff Nolan had just vacated. On a long sigh Aunt Gertie said, "Dear, I think you had a nervous breakdown."

"A nervous breakdown?"

"Yes." My aunt hesitated and took a deep breath as if the words she was about to say were difficult to bring forth. Fidgeting in her chair, she turned her face away from me and laid her hand upon her chest just over her heart. "You know that I lost my first born child?"

"Yes, my cousin Amos, had he lived."

"There never was a dearer, sweeter baby than my little Amos. When I lost him, I just could find no reason to live in this harsh world." Aunt Gertie rubbed at her moist eyes, then turned back to look closely into my eyes. "I know where you were, child - cause I've been there. It is a place to go and be healed but sooner or later life draws you back."

"Oh, Aunt Gertie," I lay my head on her soft shoulder. "I knew we were a lot alike but I never knew how much until now. Did - did you ever go back there?" A chill chased over my skin, for I didn't want to sink into that void ever again, no matter how difficult life became.

"No, dear, that is a place to rest and gain strength that will carry you through the rest of your life; you won't have to go

The Chosen Child   *Joan Hall*

there again." She caught my hand in hers, giving it a tight squeeze.

"I just couldn't fight Luke and Doyle, Aunt Gertie. When I found Chris all bloody, I just knew they had shot him. I overheard them plotting - Doyle found out that Chris was a federal agent who was searching for Luke's still."

"What?" Aunt Gertie's eyes widened in shock and her hand flew to her throat. Do you mean Doyle shot that young man? Do you know for sure? Why - why, that's murder."

"Yes - yes," I answered. "He confessed to Luke; I heard him with my own ears. I swear." I crossed my heart to emphasize my honesty. "But Luke wouldn't let me tell, he said if I reported Doyle, he would kill Papa in revenge. I just couldn't take it - I had to escape - even if it was just in my mind." Pausing, my body went limp and I sagged against my aunt, for it was a relief to finally unload all the bad things I had harbored in my head.

"Lord have mercy. I knew those Johnsons had to be up to no good. I should have realized they had too much money to have come by it honestly." Rolling her eyes upward, she shook her head in disgust. "That Doyle was always trouble. He's just too much like his Pa. If he could shoot down an innocent boy like that, then he could just as easily kill his own father. I reckon he's the one that struck Luke down and is trying to pin it on Ezra. Well, he won't get away with it."

Gertie rose purposely to her feet and stood in a rebellious pose as if she were preparing to do battle. "Just wait till I tell my boys what's going on. They'll come running. My Peter will get the truth out of that sneaky Johnson if he has to beat it out of him."

"No, no, Aunt Gertie, please - there can't be any more violence. Let's try another way."

"Well, you have to tell the sheriff. Maybe he'll realize that Ezra is not the killer around here."

"I have no proof. It's just my word against Doyle's. The sheriff will just think I'm making this up to help Papa."

"Mercy sakes." Aunt Gertie sighed and dropped back down into her chair. "What are we going to do, child?"

"I'll have to get proof some way; find the evidence that will clear Papa of Luke's killing, and get Doyle for Chris's death too."

"But how?" Her weathered face creased into a worried frown and she clutched my hands in hers. "Abby, you can't go back to that house where Doyle is living. There's no telling what he might do. Your Papa wanted you home; he was coming to get you when he found Luke."

"I have to go back, Aunt Gertie. I can't just stay here and not try to help Papa. Don't worry, Doyle and Edward think

The Chosen Child   *Joan Hall*

I'm still sick in my head which will make it easier."

"All right," my aunt agreed, "but it's against my better judgment.   I think we should let the law take care of the situation.   Even though I know Sheriff Nolan's not much for figuring out things."

On a sigh, I said, "I have a while before I have to get back to the house."

"Good," Aunt Gertie said with a lighter voice. Rising to her feet, she pulled me up also. "Come inside and visit with your brothers and sisters. They've been missing you something awful."

I checked the clock as I stepped through the kitchen door of the Johnson house and let my breath out in relief. I still could not think of it as home. The timepiece read four-thirty. I made sure I returned in time to neaten the house and have supper on before Doyle and Edward came home. The house was so quiet, the ever present rhythmic tic-tock of the mantle clock in the living room sounded clearly in my ears. Softly, I stepped into the next room. Where would be the best place for Luke's coffin? Hesitating before a tall slim table with a potted fern atop, I lifted the stand, carried it over and deposited it next to the door, clearing an expanse of floor. That would do nicely. Neighbors would be able to view him easily when they walked in.

After moving on to the bedroom I had shared with Luke, I stood before the darkened window. Hesitantly, I tugged at the paper blind, allowing it to rise and spin around the spring rod at the top of the window. The shade had been pulled down that evening I found Chris's body and had been lifted only once since by Aunt Gertie. Bright light flooded the room. Standing in the warm rays, I closed my eyes. My muscles loosened as tension slowly ebbed from my body. I hadn't realized I had been so tense.

The hours spent with the kids had done much to lighten my mood. It was hard to be morose with five pairs of young arms hugging you all at once. I tested a smile just to see how it felt. It had been so long since I had even had the urge to smile. Purposely, I tightened my lips. I would have to be careful and not let Doyle and Edward learn of my new awareness.

Sliding my gaze over my marriage bed, I saw with my mind's eye the child I had been lying huddled next to the sprawled male figure who had been my husband - no, my captor. The image would not go away. Never again would I have to endure Luke's touch. It was just too good to be true. I would have to see Luke stretched out in his casket before I could allow myself to believe.

A low rumbling of distant thunder signaled a storm was

The Chosen Child   *Joan Hall*

moving in. It was still unseasonably hot which spurned erratic storms that had plagued the area all season. Mid-September and still the temperature climbed into the mid nineties almost daily. The heat would have to break soon. I turned and peered through the window at the horizon. Blackness gathered like a mighty army readying for an assault.

Wiping the moisture from my forehead, I decided it would not be a good night, with Luke laying a corpse and a storm brewing. What if the power got knocked out? I shuddered at the thought. I had grown to appreciate the brightness of the electrified light bulb. For an instant, I regretted not doing as Aunt Gertie wanted me to do and stayed in the noisy, cheery cabin with my brothers and sisters. But that would have been an easy out, and besides, my aunt said she would be coming to pay her respects during the evening.

A whimpering just on the other side of the window drew my attention. Belle's appealing brown eyes gazed back at me. The hound wagged her tail and whined when she noted my attention. "Oh, Belle, you're afraid of the storm, aren't you. Do you want to come inside?" Belle yelped in answer.

Deciding to overrule my aversion, I rushed to the front door. The hound and I had grown to be friends, somewhat. My heart swelled with gratitude whenever I looked at the gangly dog, ever since that night someone dragged me from the porch.

The Chosen Child   *Joan Hall*

"Come on, Belle, let's get something to eat. I would much prefer taking my meal with you."

Indeed, I did not want to sit across the table from Doyle and Edward, not tonight. As the dog lapped her fare from the bowl at my feet, I let my mind ponder Luke's death, reviewing the scene I witnessed through the keyhole. There had to be a clue that would lead to proof of Doyle's guilt. Again I saw Luke retrieving his gun from the bureau and the shocked reaction of both Doyle and Edward. Could Edward be the guilty one? No, I rejected the thought, for Edward was just too gentle a soul. It had to have been Doyle. But Doyle had no feeling for Papa so why should he have tried to protect him? He wouldn't, so he must have wanted Luke dead for his own selfish reason. My logic see-sawed. I didn't know what to think or who to blame.

The distant hum of a motor vehicle interrupted my thoughts. Time had passed quickly. Hurriedly, I gulped the last bite of my stew, and then stepped into the living room. After loosening my hair a bit, I slumped into a chair. That was the way Doyle and Edward would expect to find me. A shuffle of feet followed the slam of a car door.

"Right this way, fellows," Doyle said to the two hefty men who lugged the heavy coffin, one on either side, up the porch steps. Mr. Ellis hurried in ahead of them, pushing a table on rollers. "Be careful with that precious cargo," he huffed.

"Evening, Abby - I mean Mrs. Johnson. Where would you like us to put Luke?" His voice came out in breathless gasps as if he had been rushed and was in a hurry to complete his duties. He lowered his gaze to his black oxford shoes.

I pointed. "I cleared a place for him," I said in a monotone voice. Lifting the silver colored box, the men positioned it on the table that Ellis had draped with a faded navy satin cloth.

"Uh - Abby, do you want us to open him up?" Ellis asked gently, fidgeting from one foot to another.

I hesitated. Bodies were usually shown at wakes, but I would prefer not to look upon the still form that had caused me so much grief.

"Yeah, let's open him up." Doyle spoke up, relieving me of the decision. "We will probably be having visitors soon." The hinges creaked as the lid raised, and I closed my eyes.

"Oh Pa, Pa." At Edward's wrenching wail, my eyes flashed open. He burst into tears and slumped to his knees in front of the open casket. Reacting to his grief, I rose to my feet, walked over and placed a hand on his shoulders. His sobs quieted to muffled gasps as he regained control.

Helplessly, my gaze swept to the corpse. An urge to cry assailed me. Death was so final. The loss of life, any life should be mourned. I could never hate enough to wish this end to anyone, not even Luke.

"You did a good job, Ellis. He looks right natural," Doyle said with a thickened voice as he turned to shake the mortician's hand and dismiss him.

"Let's go boys," Ellis addressed his helpers. "Maybe we can beat that storm. It's a slow mover so that means it's gaining strength." He pulled out a handkerchief and wiped at his face. "I sure hope there's cooler weather behind that there tempest."

With a shudder, I watched the men file out of the house. *Lord, help me.* I was alone with Doyle, Edward and Luke's corpse. "There's hot food in the kitchen," I said, striving for normalcy even though my heart thumped against my ribs. If I placed my shaking hand against my chest I knew I could feel each drumming beat.

"Come on, Edward," Doyle urged his brother to his feet. "We ain't eat all day."

Edward raised, his hunger overruling his grief. I dropped into my chair again, holding myself stiff and upright. I would not rest easy tonight. Belle tagged quietly behind me, then settled down at my feet. I reached down and smoothed my hand over the dog's knobby head. A faithful friend, a warm being without guile or deceit, was reassuring. Time ticked slowly but finally a rap sounded at the door. Mr. and Mrs.

Warden rushed in, followed by the Evers and the Freemans.

Mrs. Warden said, "We can't stay long, Abby. The sky is as black as pitch. A storm has been brewing for hours and it's bound to be a bad one when it hits."

"Thank you for coming," I returned. "I understand why you can't stay. Have you seen my Aunt Gertie?" Fear for my aunt's safety overruled my desire to have her reassuring presence near me.

"No dear," Mrs. Warden replied. "Perhaps she decided it was best not to come out with the sky looking the way it does."

"I hope you're right," I answered, worry gnawing at my heart.

The neighbors' visits were all brief. They tiptoed in, spoke their regrets in hushed tones, quietly looked down on Luke's remains and departed as soon as decorum allowed. I couldn't help but compare this wake with the evening my mother was open for viewing. Papa's house brimmed with folks who came laden with foods and pastries. They had talked and laughed, feeling free to be joyous in the comfortable cottage even on such a sad occasion, celebrating the life and love that had been lost.

All too soon the house grew quiet, stillness drenched with foreboding. No rustling of leaves or birdsong sounded outside, just a heavy quiet pressure, a waiting. I tugged at Belle, urging her warm alive body up to share my seat. With my arms around the hound's neck, I hung on tightly. Edward and Doyle both sat in silence, lost in their own thoughts.

The storm burst upon us like an explosion, slamming the house with a blast of hot wind. Jarring thunder and white hot lightning followed close behind. The wind screamed around the old structure and tearing gusts slammed the shutters against the walls. The light dangling from the center of the ceiling flickered, and then disappeared into darkness. Panic seized me and I in turn clutched Belle until she whined.

"Damn," Doyle growled. "We'll have to light the kerosene lamps." Endless minutes passed while he stumbled around the room. Finally, thankfully, the stroke of a match brought forth a soft glow. After capturing the flame inside a globe he turned up the wick. As the golden light rose, Doyle's dark shadow lengthened until it stretched across the room, looming over his father's casket. I closed my eyes against the raw image, reminded of the last time I saw Luke alive.

"There, Abby," Edward said in a gentle voice. Opening my eyes, I saw he had lit another lamp and placed it on the table beside my chair. The second lamp added brightness to the room, easing some of my anxiety.

I hadn't realized I had been holding my breath until a

The Chosen Child *Joan Hall*

long moan demanded escape. As the air left my lungs, I collapsed like an empty feed sack, falling back in the chair. Exhaustion drained me totally but I struggled to keep my eyes open, fighting the heaviness of my eyelids.

"Abby, you go on to bed." Edward's voice softened with concern. "We'll keep vigil tonight."

I could not refuse. Maybe sleep could blot out the raging storm. Following Edward's suggestion, I rose and stumbled across the room, motioning for Belle to follow. Once inside my bedroom, I fell against the closed door in relief, thankful to be away from the nightmare in the next room. Outside, the rain pounded the house until I feared it might be jarred from the foundation. The storm raged as if the forces from hell were loosened, the wind was screams of tormented demons pouring their vengeance upon the earth. After pushing the bolt, securing my bedroom from the rest of the house, I dropped down on the bed. Hugging Belle close, we rocked back and forth. I trembled like leaves being tossed by the tearing wind. Would the night and the storm ever pass?

Within the midst of the onslaught, a definite drumming sounded at the side window. Jerking my head up, my startled gaze flew in the direction of the intrusive noise. A pale gaunt face stared back at me. Wet hair plastered down around a pale desperate, seeking face. I stifled a scream as my heart leapt in

The Chosen Child   *Joan Hall*

terror. I dived beneath the covers and pulled them up over my head. My body quaked so the mattress moved beneath me.

"Oh Lord, help me," I cried silently. What was happening to me now? Was my mind finding another way to run from this unbearable situation? Aunt Gertie promised I would never have to go back to that strange dark void place again, but she never said anything about seeing pale ghostly faces in my terror.

The tapping sounded again and I huddled lower trying to meld with the rumpled covers so my body could not be discerned. The waxen image would go away if I lay still long enough.

Belle whimpered and her paws scratched against the bare floor as she trotted across the room. The hound yelped in a low manner as if she knew she should be secretive. The rapping came again, so I dared to lift my head and peep from under the quilts as my frantic heartbeat lowered a bit. Belle barked again. A soft cry erupted from me and I rubbed my eyes in disbelief. It couldn't be - but it was.

"Oh, Chris."

There, alive as life itself was my prince. He lifted his fingers to tap on the window, but I threw the covers away and dashed across the room. Quickly, I turned the latch that freed the window, allowing it to be raised. I reached out and touched

The Chosen Child *Joan Hall*

the young, handsome face. He was real and he was alive, although wet and his face felt cold to the touch. My heart sang in joyous relief.

"Chris - I thought you were dead. I found you," I whispered, still not willing to believe my eyes. "The body hanging over the fence - who?"

"S-h-h-h," he hushed me. "I'll explain everything later," he whispered. "I heard about Luke's death and knew I had to see you. I couldn't put it off any longer. I had to know you were okay and let you know that I was still alive."

"I'm okay now. Chris, you can't stay out in this storm," I cried as a flash of dangerous lightning crackled across the hill in the distance. "Go to the barn, you'll be safe there."

"Will you come to me?" he pleaded as his wet hands clutched mine.

"Yes, yes, I'll be right there, now go." I turned to urge Belle over to the bed. "Here girl," I said, patting the mattress, enticing the animal to jump atop the bed. "Now lie down." I pushed the dog's head down onto the pillow to let her know what was expected of her. The dog happily obliged, stretching her body out in a comfortable pose. Pulling the covers up around Belle, I arranged the blankets in a way that outlined the form and allowed only the dog's muzzle to protrude. "You stay like that and have a nice nap," I whispered, patting the dog's

The Chosen Child *Joan Hall*

back. As if on cue, Belle closed her eyes. Now if Doyle were to peek in the window during the night he would think me sound asleep.

Quickly, I retrieved a quilt from the bureau, turned down the lamp and lifted the window. The rain still pummeled in slashing sheets. Hesitating for a moment, I stood under the eave of the house after lowering the window. After shaking out the weighty quilt, I draped it over my head and dashed for the barn.

"Chris - Chris," I called into the dark structure.

"I'm here, Abby." He moved up close beside me as a bright flash of lightning illuminated his handsome youthful face.

"Oh, you're so wet," I cried. "You'll catch your death of cold. Here." I opened my arms, lifting away the heavy quilt in an offer to share its inner dry warmth. Gladly he stepped inside, pulling the generous cover around his shoulders.

My breath caught at his close proximity. A nice, clean fragrance, like soap, wafted around him. We huddled close for a moment, neither saying a word. In the next jarring shaft of lightning our eyes locked and slowly he moved his arms to encircle my waist. Lightly and gently he pulled my shivering body close, holding me against him until finally I freed my arms and wrapped them around his neck. Silently, we held each other until our shared warmth enveloped us and chased away the last chilling effects of the cold rain.

"I can't believe you're here," I breathed. "It's like a dream. I'm not dreaming, am I, Chris? I couldn't bear for this to not be real." I nestled my cheek against his, so close I could feel the fringe of his lashes as he closed his eyes.

"No, Abby, this isn't a dream," he answered breathlessly. "Come, let's sit down." He pulled me over to a rough bench.

"Tell me what happened. Who was that poor man who got shot?" The memory of my grisly discovery of the body draped over the fence tortured me. "He had blond hair just like yours."

"Yes, his name was William - William P. Manning." Chris hesitated and wiped a hand across his eyes. "He was my partner with the Internal Revenue Service. Twenty-four years old. This was his first assignment." A flash of lightning brightened Chris's face, exposing his pain. "We had just separated hours before while searching for Luke's still. I knew it had to be on the mountain somewhere. William was to search one side and I the other. I didn't get a chance to tell him I had found the operation. Luke had it well hidden."

"I'm so sorry about William."

"I had to accompany his body back to Washington. I wanted to be the one to break the news to his parents." Chris fell silent, seeming overcome with emotion. "I - I feel responsible because I was the one who talked him into joining the force." His voice grew raspy and tight as if he were fighting the urge to cry. "There had to be an autopsy and then a funeral. That's why I've been gone so long."

"My Mama - passed away - too."

"Oh, you poor baby," Chris whispered as he squeezed my hand. "I'm sorry, I heard when I got back, but I was out of town at the time of her funeral. I've been so wrapped up in my own loss I didn't think of what you had been through." Chris groaned and his voice hardened. "I swore I'd get Luke for what he's done and now I've come back to find him dead by someone else's hand."

"But - but Luke didn't shoot William - Doyle did," I said in a rush.

"What?" Chris's voice held disbelief.

"Yes, I heard him confess to Luke. He did it, he shot your partner. I couldn't tell the sheriff because Luke threatened to kill my Papa if I did. "

"Don't worry, we'll get Doyle. I have proof, a fragment of the gun stalk. After he shot William, he . . he struck him in the back of the head, I guess to make sure he was dead."

"Oh, Dear God, Doyle is a monster." I shuddered. "He has only one gun and usually keeps it hanging on the wall at the head of his bed. But I haven't seen it lately."

The Chosen Child　　　　　　　　　　　　　　　　　　　*Joan Hall*

"He probably hid it - which will make it more difficult. I've got to have the weapon for proof."

"I think Doyle killed Luke too. I know Papa didn't do it. But the sheriff thinks he did. I can't imagine who else would be so cold hearted. Aunt Gertie wanted me to come back home to live but I had to be here; I have to find the evidence to clear Papa."

"If Doyle is brutal enough to kill so recklessly, Abby, you shouldn't be near him. You could be in danger too." Chris reached out and traced his finger along my cheek, then brought it down to my lips. His voice softened, making his words feel like gentle caresses. "I couldn't stand it if you were harmed."

"I won't be," I assured him. "Doyle is not nearly as clever as he thinks himself to be." I had fooled him into thinking my mind was weakened. If I could keep up the pretense, sooner or later I would gather all the proof needed for the court. I grew more confident of my ability. Gone was the shy weak child I had been when Luke and I married, and gone was the frightened youth who sought refuge from the mental anguish of battle. I was a woman now with cleverness to rival any Johnson male. The last weeks had been tough, but I had survived. Sagging against Chris, I stifled a yawn. The strain of the day was taking its toll.

"I'm tired." I lay my head down onto Chris's shoulder.

Rain still beat the barn roof relentlessly. I did not relish running through the downpour to get back to the house nor did I want to go back inside that hurtful place.

"I think I'll stay here in the barn until the storm passes," Chris said, "and sneak out before daylight."

"Come." Grabbing his hand, I pulled him to his feet. "Follow me, I'll show you the hay loft. You can rest there; the hay is very comfortable." Feeling my way along the stalls, I found the ladder that led to the upper level. Lifting the heavy quilt away from my legs, I climbed the rungs with Chris following close behind. We dropped down on the soft fragrant mound of straw. I ran my hands through the golden hay, plumping it into a soft pallet.

Chris fell down beside me. After stretching out, he breathed, "M-m-m, this is nice." I spread the quilt over him. "Will you stay with me for awhile? No one will ever know you're gone," he whispered, a longing in his voice. Could I refuse? A lightning flash illuminated his soft pleading eyes. His brief smile tore at my heart. Hesitating, I noted the rain had slackened to a steady hard rhythm. The worst of the storm had passed. I could easily get back to the house without getting drenched. Belle should be sleeping peacefully in the big bed. The straw and Chris were much more appealing. I pictured Edward and Doyle sitting in the living room keeping vigil with

The Chosen Child *Joan Hall*

Luke's corpse, and shuddered. Gingerly, I lay back down on the hay beside Chris. He shared the cover, pulling it up over my waist. We lay quietly without touching but he was close enough for me to feel his breath fanning my cheek. Turning slightly, I breathed his soft breath into me. The rain had finally slowed to a steady patter. The tapping on the tin roof turned musical and soothing. Contentment settled in my heart, a feeling made foreign because it had been so long since I had felt the blessed emotion. I would close my eyelids just for a little while I decided.

Chris wasn't dead. He was lying here next to me. I still couldn't believe and reached to touch him. He caught my hand and held it tight then whispered, "I can't believe I'm here with you like this. You know - when I first saw you in the pond that day - you looked like a fairy princess."

How could our minds have been so parallel, I wondered, catching my breath. It seemed he mirrored my every thought. Did he also share my feelings as well, this strange new stirring in my heart, this new ache to be close to him? I moved, bringing my length tight against him and he circled me with his arm. He brought his lips against the curve of my neck and I moaned. For an instant, I thought of my marriage and started to pull away. I'm a widow now, I reminded myself. Slowly I turned my body to face him.

The Chosen Child   *Joan Hall*

"Oh, Abby," he groaned, and then covered my mouth with his. His hands caressed my back with soft movements. An unfamiliar sweet ache began to build inside me, growing with each stroke. I called out his name in a ragged whisper and he clutched me closer. Closing my eyes tight, I succumbed to Chris and the warmth flooding through my body. I closed my mind, for now, I would not worry about my Papa's dire circumstance nor my own.

Chapter Thirteen

The storm broke the merciless grip of the summer heat. Shivering, I pulled the cover up close beneath my chin. Early rays of sunshine filtered through the cracks of the barn. Memory flooded my mind and I turned quickly to where Chris lay. The space beside me was empty but I could still see the imprint of his body. I hadn't been dreaming. Chris was real. For an instant I had doubted the events of the night. Could we have really made love? The softness in my heart told me we had. Finally, I had experienced love, and I liked the way it made me feel.

"Oh, it must be close to seven," I groaned as my heart tripped in alarm. I knew I must get back to the house before Doyle discovered that I was not in my bed. During the early hours, the sky had cleared to a cloudless state. Taking the time to draw a deep fresh breath, I decided it would be a good day to lay Luke to rest. The force of the storm had strewn the yard with fallen limbs and debris but the structures had weathered well. Except for a loosened shutter and a dangling strip of roofing, the house appeared much the same.

Cowering low, I scurried back to the window I had exited the night before. Belle lay sprawled on top of the covers, not quite as I had left her the night before. I had feared Doyle peeking through the small space around the blind of the window during the night. There was easy access to one window from the front porch. Since it had been a dark night Belle would have confused the scene. Surely my absence would not have been noted.

Belle stirred to life and seemed anxious to leave the room. Quietly I slipped the latch on the door. Doyle and Edward still sat in their chairs, one at either end of Luke's coffin. Edward's head lay to the side, almost resting on the casket. Doyle's had dropped forward. Both were soundly sleeping. My heart wrenched at the sight, but I would not let sympathy rule. Doyle was a murderer and who knew what else.

No, I would not allow my heart to dictate my actions, not even for Edward.

Without conscious thought, my eyes flew to the still figure lying on the satin bed. In the bright morning light Luke appeared as if he might just be sleeping. Many mornings I had stared at that same profile. By instinct, my body recoiled and I took a step backwards. Luke was dead but he still could cause my heart to thump in anxious fear.

"Abby," Edward exclaimed as he stirred to life. Stretching his hands above his head, he twisted his torso in an obvious effort to ease his sore muscles. Paleness marred his face and his hair stuck out in disarray. "Man, what a night," he groaned. "I swear that storm was born in the depths of hell."

"It just made the night more interesting. Pa's spirit was ushered out in proper style," Doyle stated in a low, measured tone. I darted him a quick glance, wondering how long he had been awake and how observant he had been. Had he noticed my even gait and clear eyes?

"The storm has broken the heat," I said, lowering my gaze to stare at the floor. "It's quite cool this morning."

"Did you sleep well, Abby?" Doyle's voice held an edge of steel.

Holding my composure, even though my heart leapt into my throat, I replied, "Yes, Belle kept me company. She's a good dog."

Doyle pulled himself to his feet, strode across the room then lifted back the curtain and stared intently out the window. "It's going to be a fine day for a funeral. We're laying Pa to rest at one o'clock, Abby." He turned, directing his gaze toward me. "Pa wasn't fond of long drawn-out memorials so we're keeping it simple with a grave-side service." To his brother, he said, "Edward, you go and make sure Ellis's helpers dug Pa's grave proper and see if that storm flooded the hole. Me and Abby need to have a talk."

I held my breath as Edward strode from the house. What was Doyle up to now? Clearing his throat, he ran his fingers through his hair then came directly to the point. "Uh - Abby, the sheriff knows who killed Pa. Ezra did it."

Feigning a gasp, I dropped into a chair. "No, Papa wouldn't hurt a flea," I said, not allowing a strong show of emotion.

"It had to be him, the evidence is too strong." I didn't answer and kept my face in an unresponsive pose.

"I guess you'll be staying on here with me and Edward with your Pa in jail and all."

"I guess so," I agreed as if I had no other choice.

"Now that Pa is gone, I will be running the place - uh - since I'm the oldest." Doyle seemed to be measuring his words,

The Chosen Child   *Joan Hall*

trying them on, like a young man striving to fit into his father's clothes. He cleared his throat and continued, "I'll be making all the decisions now."

With hesitation, he gave me a beseeching stare and wavered. "I know I shouldn't have shot that young man, Abby. I'm not really a bad person. I just thought it was what Pa wanted, and besides, he was trespassing on Johnson property and poking his nose where he had no business. He could have dropped his gun - it could have been an accident."

I sat in silence not justifying his words with a reply, staring at him with cold deadened eyes. Let him try to salve his conscious; it did not lessen the severity of his crime. Pacing the floor in front of me, he glanced first to his father's corpse then back to me. Finally he burst, his voice a menacing growl.

"Do you remember what Pa said about you telling on me?" At my blank stare, he grated, "I ain't going to jail; a man might as well be dead as to rot in prison, and if I go I'll take everybody around me too." His eyes held a fire that burned a hole through my heart. "Do you understand me, Abby? Can you get that into your crazy head?" He squatted in front of me and pushed his face close to mine. "Do you want to be responsible for that? There would be more blood on your hands, girl." He paused to let his words sink in, then his eyes brightened with the glint of steel at his next thought. "If you tell on me, I'll kill you too. Yeah, I'll make sure you keep your mouth shut one way or another."

I squeezed my eyes tightly closed and leaned backward in the chair. I could swear that Luke still held me in his iron grip. He just had a younger face and a different name.

The slam of the screen door diverted Doyle's hard gaze. "Everything looks pretty good, just a little muddy," Edward said as he stepped through the front door. His eyes poured over the two of us and a concerned frown creased his forehead. "What's going on?"

"Me and Abby were just talking," Doyle said as he pushed himself to his feet. "She needed to know a few things."

"You told her about Ezra's arrest, didn't you?" Edward accused, tightening his hands into coiled fists and taking a threatening step toward his brother. "You know she's not well, she don't need any more bad news right now. She needs peace."

"The truth never hurt anybody." Doyle turned mocking, cruel eyes on me. "She can't get any worse than she is right now. Look at her, she's like a wounded turtle. Just touch her and she pulls herself back inside a shell and closes it up tight." Throwing his head back, Doyle laughed, finding humor in his hurtful words. Edward didn't join in, but kept his face in a stiff, accusing frown. Doyle was not deterred and bellowed his laughter as he strode from the room.

Edward dropped to his knees beside me and patted my shoulder. "I won't let Ezra go to prison, so don't you worry about it. There's been enough evil done around this place. It has to stop. The jailing of an innocent man won't be added to the list of crimes committed here."

His words tumbled around in my head. He must know that Doyle killed their father. Dare I speak up and try to convince him to go to Papa's aid and tell the sheriff what Doyle had done? He would realize I had been faking my mindless state. Would I be able to persuade him to speak out? If Edward were so concerned, then why did he not report the murder of the revenue agent? I lifted my gaze to meet his troubled dark eyes and hesitated, unable to bring myself to speak. Edward's eyes appeared weak. Having a sense of wrong doing and displaying the courage to right that wrong were two different matters. For now, I decided to continue the charade. Maybe I would prod though and get him to make a slip of his tongue.

"Did Luke suffer?" I asked with a wringing of my hands. "I don't like suffering."

"Uh, no, Abby, he didn't suffer," Edward answered then quickly added. "I gathered from what the sheriff said that he was knocked unconscious so he didn't know he was dying. It was probably a peaceful death."

For a minute, I thought Edward had been a witness to

the act. "He can't hurt you now, that's over, so you can stop being afraid. You can get well, can't you?" His gaze probed mine.

How much could I say and not risk my cover? Perhaps I could spurn a confrontation between the brothers in order to force out the truth. "No, Luke can't hurt me anymore, but Doyle can," I whispered, rolling my eyes in the direction Doyle had exited, trying for an expression of apprehension. "He has a big gun and he kills with it," I added, covering my face with my hands. This action wasn't pretend. The vision of the bloody body I had found still brought shivers to my skin.

"Doyle's big gun is gone. He can't use it anymore. I hid the damn thing, and only I know where it is, so he won't hurt you with it."

My head snapped up in attention and I almost asked him where he put the weapon before caution halted my tongue. "He can kill with a rock too," I said, watching Edward closely for his reaction.

Recoiling, Edward pulled away from me. I had gone too far. "Doyle is my brother, Abby, the only kin I got left in the world. He's not the best, but he don't hurt helpless females." A long sigh escaped him. "I'd better go. There's a lot I got to do today." With his last statement he shuffled wearily from the room. The information I gleaned from the conversation wasn't much but at least it was a start.

Preacher Allison stood at the head of Luke's grave site, his arms folded across the Bible he clutched to his chest. Patiently, he stood waiting for the handful of folks straggling in to stand in respectful silence around the hole. Aunt Gertie met me halfway down the lane to walk the remaining distance together.

"I missed you last evening, Aunt Gertie," I whispered beneath my breath, lifting a white crochet shawl higher on my head to partially hide my face.

"I'm sorry, honeychild. I meant to be here for you but the kids were frightened by that awful storm that brewed all afternoon. I had to make a choice, dear, and they needed me so badly. I just prayed and fretted all night that you would be okay. You were all right, weren't you?" my aunt inquired with a scowl of worry on her dear face. She patted my back.

Thinking of the night spent lying in Chris's arms up in the hay loft, I said, "Yes, I was fine." Again, I heard the spattering of rain on the tin barn roof and a heat flooded through me, warming my cheeks.

"I have to tell you something, Aunt Gertie," I murmured, barely able to conceal the excitement within me. My aunt pulled me close and urged my head down on her shoulder in a show of comfort, so I could whisper in her ear.

With eyes widening, Aunt Gertie pulled back and cried aloud. "What? Alive?" Catching herself, as heads turned in our direction, she quickly stammered, "There - there - don't cry," as a cover for her outburst.

"He came to me last night during the storm."

Aunt Gertie stared at me with pity in her eyes. "Abby, dear, I know you were most upset at the loss of your young friend, and last night must have been a terrible ordeal." She shook her head and clucked her tongue. "Oh, I should have found a way to get here and be a support to you."

"I didn't dream him. He was real, he was real, I swear. At first I was frightened. His face at the window appeared so pale that I thought he was a ghost. But Chris is definitely alive." At Aunt Gertie's doubtful stare, I added, "I touched him; he held me."

At the smile lighting my aunt's face, I knew she was convinced. "That's wonderful, dear," she said, "one bright spot in this dreadful situation. Oh, but who was the poor boy who was killed?"

"Chris's partner, his name was William. Chris was very upset."

"And rightfully so," my aunt raved. "That Doyle has to be brought to justice." We hushed our voices when we reached

The Chosen Child *Joan Hall*

the small solemn gathering.

Preacher Allison waited for total silence before he started the service. Beginning the eulogy, he said, "We are gathered here today to say goodbye to Luke Johnson, a husband, a father, a neighbor and a friend."

A friend? Preacher Allison's words haunted me. I let my gaze move over the solemn faces of the small group. It seemed decent folks would come and show respect to a family in mourning, no matter what the circumstance. Everyone gathered there knew of the conflict between my Papa and Luke, probably knew my father had been arrested for killing Luke. They also knew Luke to be an overbearing, hard, unsympathetic tyrant. Yet they came and spoke kind words to his sons and honored his passing with a quiet dignity.

The service ended only moments after it began with the preacher tossing a clump of damp soil onto the coffin. "Into thine hands we deliver Luke's spirit, Lord. Please judge him kindly. Amen."

"I'd like for you to stay awhile, Aunt Gertie," I pleaded, turning from the grave. She walked beside me as we headed toward the house. Lowering our heads, we felt free to continue our discussion of the turn of events.

"What can I do to help you and Chris?" Gertie asked, her voice strong with the ring of determination.

The Chosen Child   *Joan Hall*

"We have to find Doyle's gun, the one he used to kill William. Edward hid it somewhere." Searching my aunt's eyes, I asked, "Are you sure you want to get involved in this? It might be dangerous. Doyle swore he would not go to prison." It was good to have someone to aid in my dilemma, but I couldn't stand for harm to come to my dear aunt.

Wiping a hand over her wrinkled brow, Aunt Gertie's face glowed pink with excitement and she blurted, "I ain't never seen a man yet that could make me cower in fear, even a Johnson. If it's my time to fall then I can't think of a better way to go than helping out the people I love."

"Oh Aunt Gertie." I smiled at her flair for dramatics and gave her a big hug. Her attitude gave me strength.

As we stepped through the doorway of the house, I glanced over my shoulder to make sure Edward and Doyle were as we had left them. They stood yet at the grave site speaking with the preacher while workmen shoveled dirt, filling Luke's grave.

"Now, where would a man hide a shotgun?" Aunt Gertie asked aloud as she scratched her head thoughtfully.

"Maybe he dropped it into the well," I suggested searching my own brain.

"No man would put a good gun where it would come to harm, it just ain't natural, no-sir-re-bob."

The Chosen Child   *Joan Hall*

Nodding at her logic, I stooped to peer under the couch and then the buffet. Pausing at the steps that led to the second story, my aunt said, "You watch for them two and I'll search the bedrooms upstairs."

"Oh, Aunt Gertie, I don't know if that's a good idea." Glancing out the door, I saw that the two men still stood as they had moments before. "You might get caught," I whispered turning back to face her. Aunt Gertie had disappeared from view. "Be with us, Lord," I prayed as I began a search of the kitchen and pantry. Precious moments slipped away while I peeked behind basins and in churns.

Doyle's rough voice jarred me upright. "Did you lose something?" Struggling to remain calm, I turned to face the brothers.

"I - I can't find my griddle - it's gone," I stammered helplessly.

"Heck, can't you remember anything?" Doyle complained shortly. "The griddle hangs on the back of the stove." With a glance about the kitchen, his eyes narrowed warily. "Where's Gert?" he demanded. "I saw her come in here with you."

My gaze flew in the direction of the stairs, where I could view the first few steps. The hem of Aunt Gertie's blue dotted swiss dress floated into view. Gasping loudly, I cried, "She had to go to the outhouse. Aunt Gertie went to the outhouse," I repeated. A sigh of relief escaped me as my aunt's dress disappeared back up the stairs.

"Well, it's done. Pa's been put to rest," Edward said in a strained, hurting voice. Exhaustion etched his face and dark blotches hung beneath his eyes. This had not been easy for him. His appearance seemed much the same as it had when his mother died. "Don't bother cooking, Abby, we'll just have leftovers. I just ain't in no mood to eat."

The slam of the back door drew our attention as my aunt strode in. Wisps of her grey hair flew astray and a noticeable tear marred her good dress. She had to have crawled out a window and shimmied down the elm tree that grew close to the house.

Staring coldly at the older woman, Doyle's eyes filled with open dislike. "Gert, you can go on home. Ain't no use in you hanging around. We would rather be alone in our sorrow."

His voice, so curt and dismissive, shocked me. How dare he speak in such a tone with no regard to Aunt Gertie's feelings. Anger seethed within me, but I could not speak out and give away my cover.

Acting as if she didn't recognize the open scorn in his voice, my aunt replied in a firm unrelenting voice, "I intend to spend the rest of the day and night with Abby. I've already told

The Chosen Child   *Joan Hall*

the kids not to expect me till tomorrow."

"We don't have a spare bedroom," Doyle said in a rock hard voice, not giving in.

Pulling herself up to her most daunting five foot six frame, Aunt Gertie replied, "Well then, I'll just have to stretch out on the couch I reckon." Doyle hesitated, unsure of how to handle this challenge to his new authority. Fear hovered fleetingly in his gaze.

"Maybe it's best if Gert stayed to keep Abby company," Edward prodded. "You know we got a lot to do today."

"Yeah, I guess so," Doyle reluctantly agreed. Fidgeting, he stared at me with unease in his eyes. "Gert, don't you go paying any mind to what Abby might go telling you. She's been imagining all kinds of things ever since that young man accidentally shot himself." Doyle anxiously stuck his hands into the pockets of his jeans as if he didn't know what to do with them. "It was a real shock finding him like that - all bloody and all."

Nodding her head in mock agreement, Aunt Gertie said, "Abby has had a lot of bad stuff in her life lately. It's no wonder she's sickly. I reckon any girl would collapse under the weight she's had to carry on her shoulders. I won't pay no mind to her foolishness."

Doyle visibly relaxed. Being the object of conversation

did not set easy with me, but I kept my eyes downcast without responding but how I would have liked to yell in Doyle's smug face, "I am not crazy."

"You boys go ahead and do whatever you need to do," my aunt said, using her hands to hurry them from the kitchen in a manner she would with small children. "Grab your sandwich and go, I'll help Abby gather Luke's things together for disposal. I expect you'll want to burn his clothes since they're too big for either of you." Neither male responded to Aunt Gertie's unintentional cutting remark, just stared at her, not knowing quite how to cope with her take-over manner. "We'll put his personal things in a box for you too keep."

"Whew," Aunt Gertie breathed after the two males exited through the back door. "We're going to have to work fast. I don't trust that Doyle one bit. There's meanness in his eyes the like of which I've never seen. He won't be pushed, Abby. We got to be mighty careful."

A slight knocking sounded at the front door. Peering through the screen door was a round white topped head.

"Preacher Allison," I cried in surprise. I had completely forgotten about the man who had just performed the funeral service, assuming he had left with the others. He stood as usual with his Bible clutched to his chest. "Won't you come in," I said, rushing to open the door wide. "I'm sorry I didn't realize

The Chosen Child   *Joan Hall*

you were still here."

"I just came up to the house to express to you my regrets." The preacher clucked his tongue in sympathy. "First your dear mother left and now your husband's gone on too. The Lord works in mysterious ways, dear. Ways we may not understand."

Peeking out the door behind him, I saw that everyone else had left. The preacher's horse and wagon alone were tied to the railing by the lane.

"Could I bother you for a drink of water? I forgot to bring along a canteen." He coughed to illustrate his dry condition.

"Come right into the kitchen, Preacher," Aunt Gertie said as she walked over and took the man by the arm in a familiar fashion. "I'll get that water for you. Have you had lunch?" she asked as was her habit when anyone visited close to mealtime, fully expecting him to say he couldn't hold a bite.

"As a matter of fact, I think I forgot lunch. I didn't have much time to prepare Luke's eulogy, I'm afraid I put my duties above my own selfish needs." He rolled his gaze around the kitchen, sweeping the stove and cabinets in an obvious plea.

"Abby didn't prepare lunch, but I saw biscuits and ham in the warming bin." My aunt offered what we had.

"That sounds wonderful." The old man pulled out a

The Chosen Child   *Joan Hall*

chair and plopped his round body down and stared at the two of us in an expectant manner.

My aunt and I exchanged furtive glances then she went about preparing a plate for our guest. Our plans would have to be postponed temporarily.

"I've been praying for Ezra." the preacher said in a quiet voice. "I know a man has his limits, but I just don't think he has it in him to be that violent." He scratched his chin thoughtfully. "Something just ain't right about this whole situation."

"Of course Papa didn't kill Luke." I couldn't help but defend my father. I would declare his innocence to the world if possible.

"Do you have any idea who would do such a thing?" the preacher prodded us before he bit into his biscuit sandwich.

Aunt Gertie shrugged her shoulders in approval and said, "Why not," to my questioning glance at her. What harm could come from sharing our knowledge and suspicions with Preacher Allison? We could use another ally.

"Yes, we have a definite idea of who killed Luke," I exclaimed, leaning over close to his ear and lowering my voice to a secretive whisper.

Laying down his half eaten sandwich, the preacher's eyes grew round. He reached for his Bible and pulled it close.

"There's evil in this house, Preacher," Aunt Gertie said.

The Chosen Child *Joan Hall*

"Bad people have been doing bad things. Are - are you sure you want to get involved?"

"Yes, you two ladies don't have to stand alone in this trial. Tell me what you know and maybe I can help." He reached out and grasped each of our hands sealing the unusual alliance. I smiled; I always knew Preacher Allison was a hero.

The three of us sat in silence while Preacher Allison mused over all that he had heard. After long thoughtful moments, he spoke. "The Lord must have directed me today. It was so unusual for me to skip lunch and I always pack a jug of water when I travel. He put me here in the midst of this melee for a reason, so I guess I'd better give you my services." Pausing again, he folded his hands and lowered his head in a quick prayer. "It seems the best thing we could do is find that shotgun of Doyle's," he stated, rising to his feet.

"You're a man . . ." Aunt Gertie began, but a chuckle from the preacher cut her off before she could finish.

"I was the last time I looked in the mirror," the preacher said, lightening the mood.

"As a man," my aunt tried again, giving him a disdainful frown, "where would you choose to hide a weapon so no one would find it?"

"It would have to be a dry place with space enough so the gun wouldn't get scarred," he said in a sure voice. "We males are very proud of our firearms and go to great lengths to care for them."

"We appreciate your help, sir, but that could be a hundred places in this big house, "Aunt Gertie complained.

"Well, maybe we should just search. If each of us takes a room we could go over this place thoroughly in no time," he suggested.

"Okay," my aunt said, taking authority. "I'll take the bedroom, Abby, you search the living room. Preacher, you can start in the dining area." We each hurried to our appointed rooms.

Glancing around the area I was to search, I tried to concentrate on places large enough to accommodate the stock and barrel of a gun. I had peeked under the sofa earlier. Maybe one of the bureau drawers was the hiding place. It was probably much too obvious a place but I had to search somewhere. Starting at the bottom I worked my way up the five drawers. An assortment of mostly unneeded household items and old photographs littered each drawer. The top one held linens, scarves and throws. Hurriedly, I raced my hand through the crisp cottons. When my fingers touched cold steel, I recoiled. Had I found the evidence so easily? No, the weapon was much too small. Gingerly I pulled the heavy pistol from the cabinet. I recognized the revolver as the same firearm Luke had held on the day when he was leaving to confront Papa. As I started to place the gun back where I had found it, a sudden stirring in my brain stopped me. There was something significant in this gun. Searching my mind, I relived the evening that brought me back to full conscious thought. Luke had pulled the pistol and took it with him that night, so how did it end up back in the drawer?

"Aunt Gertie, Preacher Allison, come quickly."

"Did you find it?" they asked, their voices blending, as each rushed into the room from different directions.

"No, but this is just as important," I exclaimed. "This is the gun that Luke took with him when he went to confront Papa. Sheriff Nolan didn't mention a gun. I'm sure he would have kept it in evidence if it had still been at the scene."

Aunt Gertie reached out and touched the shiny black barrel. "This means that Doyle was there with his Pa. He took the gun from Luke and brought it back to the house. Luke had to be unconscious for Doyle to manage to get his gun."

"You were right, Gertie," the preacher said in a saddened voice. "There is evil in this house. That young man was going to let Ezra go to prison for the crime he committed. Well, we're not going to let him get away with it."

I didn't want to hold the instrument of death any longer. Hurriedly, I placed it back in the drawer. "Careful with that thing," the preacher said. "It's loaded all around."

The Chosen Child   *Joan Hall*

"Did either of you have any luck in your search?" I asked.

"No." Aunt Gertie's expression fell. "I tore the bedroom upside down, looking for that shotgun."

The preacher wandered about the room with his hands clasped behind his back. His steps echoed hollowly on the plank floor. Suddenly he stopped his pacing and his gaze moved upward. "I know where Edward put that gun."

"Where? Where?" I demanded.

"Just follow me." His voice rose with excitement as he headed for the stairway. Upstairs, was a landing, then bedrooms on either side. "Which room belongs to Edward?" the old man asked.

"This one," I answered, pointing to the smallest of the rooms. It was also the neatest room in the house. I never had to clean after Edward. Even the photograph of his parents that rested on the nightstand always appeared dusted and set at a perfect angle facing his bed. It must have been the last thing he looked at before he turned out the light.

"Walk about the room and look for a loose floor board or one that has been marred." He pushed his spectacles up the bridge of his nose and bent forward to better his view. Moments later, he cried out, "I found it, I found the loose plank. It's here; I just know it's here." His voice rose in excitement as

The Chosen Child   *Joan Hall*

if his discovery might be the saving grace for his own life. He dropped down on his knees, slowly worked the board loose and pulled it away from the flooring. With his hand stretched back just out of sight, he exclaimed in a strained voice, "I got it, I got the evidence."

"Thank goodness," I cried. "We've got to get the gun to Chris right away. He needs it."

"My horse and wagon are already hitched. We can be in town in about an hour." The old man brushed off the knees of his trousers, then stood at his tallest. "Sheriff Nolan will be impressed with what we've got to show him." He lifted the gun in victory.

"Come on," Aunt Gertie urged, "I won't rest easy till we hand that darn thing over to the sheriff."

I led the way back down the stairs with quick steps. The preacher followed close behind with the heavy weapon clutched in both hands and my aunt behind him.

Chapter Fourteen

"Thought you could outsmart me, didn't you?" The harsh growling voice brought our three figures to an abrupt halt. My heart dropped like a heavy weight into the pit of my stomach. Doyle held an angry stance with his hands braced on his hips. If the hate shooting from his eyes was a tangible thing, I would have been slain right there.

"See," he said to Edward, who huddled behind him. "I told you she was a conniving little bitch. There ain't nothing wrong with her head now."

Disbelief filled Edward's eyes and he spewed accusing

words at me. "You were just pretending to be sick so you could snoop behind our backs. How could you deceive us like that, Abby?"

My body began to shake in nervous reaction. I couldn't deny my trickery. "Just for awhile, Edward," I breathlessly choked through trembling lips. "It was the only way. Doyle killed an innocent man. He should pay for his crimes." Aunt Gertie and the preacher stood quietly behind me. I did note a low murmuring from the preacher's lips, probably a prayer.

"Let us pass, boys," Preacher Allison said as he stepped around me, edging toward the door. He clutched the gun tighter. His round cheeks flushed a bright hue and his eyes danced, betraying his anxious state.

"Do you really think I'm going to let you go so you can send me to prison?" Doyle laughed, a scathing chortle, his face showing disbelief. "I know Abby's been playing me for a fool, but that's over, now we'll see who the fool is." He turned and prodded Edward with his hand. "Go get that gun."

Edward hesitated, his eyes flashing with uncertainty, then with a tightening of his jaw, strode over and easily jerked the gun from the old man's resisting arms. "I'm sorry, Preacher," he said.

"What are you going to do with us?" Aunt Gertie asked, raising her chin to stare directly into Doyle's maddened eyes.

The Chosen Child   *Joan Hall*

"Whatever I do will be your own fault, you old biddy. You had no business butting into a Johnson affair. This didn't concern you or the preacher." He turned his wrath on me. "See what you've done," he screamed, his face twisted with rage. "You've gone and got your aunt and the reverend in trouble. You've just never learned to keep your place. I knew we would rue the day Pa laid his hand on you; I just knew it. You're a curse, that's what you are, a curse of the devil with your tempting innocent face."

Doyle fell silent as if he had run out of hurtful words. Finally, after a moment he said to Edward, "We need some rope to tie them up,"

"We can't let them do that to us," my aunt whispered. "That gun wasn't loaded; we can make a run for it. They won't be able to stop all three of us."

"I agree with Gertie," the preacher said beneath his breath.

We had to do something, I decided. My Papa's life depended on our actions. "All right, let's go," I agreed. We dashed for the door with the preacher in front. His age and size slowed his gait, thwarting our chance of escape.

"Stop them," Doyle yelled as he made a grab for me. "Help me, Edward." He caught my wrist in a vice-like grip. I turned and slammed the point of my shoe against his leg, bringing a yelp of pain from him.

"Hold it, don't anybody move." Edward's threat brought us all to a stop, even Doyle. Edward stood with his hands gripped around Luke's pistol. The bureau drawer hung ajar at his hurried opening. His hands shook and his chest heaved with frantic breathing.

"Oh no," I groaned aloud. This couldn't be. Edward knew Luke's pistol was back in the drawer. The implication brought tears to my eyes. Had I been so wrong about him? I had thought him different from his brother and father, had thought him to be gentle and kind. I stilled my resistance and my two comrades followed suit.

"There's rope hanging on the back porch; get it for me," Doyle barked at his brother as he pulled the firearm from his frozen hands. Edward obeyed without objection.

Doyle held the gun pointed at a deadly aim. "Blood is thicker than water," he sneered at me when Edward left the room.

In numbed acceptance, I stood with my hands behind my back as Edward looped the rope around my wrists. What else could I do? When it was her turn, Aunt Gertie resisted. "You won't get away with this. You'll pay one way or another, if not by the law then my sons. They'll hunt you down . . ."

"Shut up or I'll tape your mouth," Doyle grated.

The Chosen Child   *Joan Hall*

When we were bound, Edward demanded of his brother, "Now what do we do?"

"We have to destroy our stash of liquor and the still." Doyle rubbed his hand across his sweating face. "We're in enough trouble without the charge of bootlegging." His eyes raked over us. "We can't leave them here; they might find a way to get free. I guess we'll just have to take them with us. Put my shotgun in the car." he ordered, "I ain't giving up my gun till I have to."

With the barrel of his pistol, he urged us through the kitchen toward the back door. Preacher Allison spotted his Bible lying on the table where he had left it. "My Bible," he pleaded, his voice breaking. "I always keep my Bible with me."

"Here," Doyle grabbed the book from the table with a sneer. Pulling loose the top opening of the preacher's shirt, he crammed it down beneath the cloth. "You can keep it right over your heart," he smirked.

Moving in single file, we followed the path that I had playfully explored weeks ago, although it seemed like years. Was I that same naive girl? I actually felt like a different person. Was this what growing up did to you, or was it the circumstance of my life that made me lose all traces of childhood? Whatever the reason, I knew it would never be recaptured.

"I feel like a turkey, all trussed up for Sunday dinner," Aunt Gertie grated, tugging her arms against the binding at her wrists.

"S-h-h-h, Aunt Gertie," I hushed her. "Don't make Doyle any more upset than he is already." The ground had been softened by the rain of the night before and made our passage up the incline difficult. More than once, I had to stop and tug my shoe from the spongy earth that sucked at my feet. At least we were leaving an obvious trail for anyone who might happen to search for us.

Finally we reached the summit. In spite of the bright sunlight, a chill wind blew over the ridge tops, a wind that rarely dipped into the sheltered hollows. Pausing to catch my breath, I worried about my older companions. My aunt seemed none the worse for the climb but the preacher's breath came in quick wheezing gasps and his cheeks bloomed with color.

"Keep moving," Doyle prodded. "It must be three o'clock already."

"Maybe they could rest for just a minute," Edward suggested in a weak voice. "That was quite a climb."

"No, we got to be packed and out of here before dark. It will be a long ride to Tennessee." He motioned with the hand gripping the gun. "Go on, Abby, you know the way."

As we trekked around the pond where I had first met

The Chosen Child   *Joan Hall*

Chris, I gazed at the clear still water, my mind reliving that day. If only I could have foreseen the future, I would have begged him to whisk me away. So many lives would have been better. But if I could have known events to come I never would have married Luke in the first place. If only I had been older and wiser. Dropping my head, I reminded myself, I hadn't been wise and I hadn't been whisked away and I was in big trouble.

"What do you want us to do now," I asked when we reached the site of the illegal operation.

"You all stand close together right over there where I can keep an eye on you and don't anybody try anything funny." Doyle indicated a clearing as he spoke, then stuck the pistol beneath the belt of his jeans.

"After we're through here what are you going to do with them?" Edward asked with an uneasy frown clouding his face.

"That all depends on how much trouble they are," Doyle growled.

"I won't let you kill them, Doyle. That stranger was a different matter. This is Abby and her aunt and our preacher." Edward spoke in lowered tones but his words carried easily to our ears. For a moment Doyle pondered our fate, his eyes sweeping from one to another. Finally he spoke in a sure hard voice.

"I think I'll leave Gert and the preacher tied here to a

tree. They'll be found in time if they're lucky." Doyle's eyes hovered on me, "but Abby, wherever I go, she goes." His voice had a ring of finality that Edward didn't question. "You take that still apart," he instructed his brother, "and I'll spill the store of liquor."

He picked up a mallet and began beating at the barrels of liquid lined along the hillside beneath the protection of a rock ledge. Noisily, Edward tore at the copper kettle until nothing was left but scrap metal, then he turned to beat at the rock hearth until nothing was left but rubble. Doyle had just delivered the final blow needed to burst the last barrel of alcohol. The clear liquid sloshed out, wetting his jeans from the knees down. "It's done," he declared, leaning on the handle of his hammer to catch his breath.

No one heard the rustle in the bush and it wasn't clear who noticed first. All heads seemed to turn at the same time. The noise the brothers made had blocked out all other sound, not allowing them to hear the intruders approach. Doyle pulled his gun as his gaze flashed to the nearby woods while Edward stood so still he seemed cast in stone.

"Throw down your weapon." The command preceded the appearance of Sheriff Nolan. He stepped into the clearing, brandishing his own gun.

"Thank the Lord," Aunt Gertie cried. "We're saved."

The Chosen Child   *Joan Hall*

Sagging in relief, I seconded my aunt's words.

Following close behind the Sheriff was Chris and Papa. When I saw my father, I squealed in wonder and started to rush toward him.

"Hold it right there, Abby," Doyle thundered. Rage emblazoned his face. "Don't take another step," he commanded, his gaze piercing me.

"It's all over, Doyle." The sheriff said in a calm manner. "Lay the gun down and come quietly with me. We have a search warrant, and we have your shotgun. We know you killed that federal agent. I'm a kindly soul and turn my head at a few things, but I don't take to murder."

"What are we going to do?" Edward turned desperate pleading eyes to his brother.

"Shut up," Doyle screamed. Desperation shone in his pale eyes. He swung his aimed gun from the sheriff to Chris and Papa then on to me and my companions.

"We got you, Johnson," Chris spoke up. "You're under arrest for the murder of William P. Manning. We came with a search warrant and found your shotgun in your car."

"You've got some answering to do about your Pa's death too," Sheriff Nolan added.

Edward collapsed under the damning words and pleaded with his brother, "Give them the gun, Doyle. We're done for."

"No," Doyle thundered. Turning his anguished face in my direction he growled like a caged animal, "You, you're the cause of all of this. When you married Pa everything started going wrong. We were fine before you showed up." He wiped the back of his hand across his face in jerky spasms. "I ain't going to prison," he declared in a voice hard and resolute.

"Put down the gun," the sheriff said, desperation creeping into his voice.

"No," Doyle retaliated. He fixed his eyes on me in a stabbing unblinking stare. My heart pounded in a frantic rhythm and fear held me in a frozen stance. "I ain't going to prison," he repeated. His words held an edge of steel. "I warned you, Abby, I warned you."

"Put down the gun," the sheriff demanded, his voice tight with tension.

"No," Doyle grated, not wavering in his stabbing unblinking stare.

"Don't be foolish, son," Papa spoke finally in a familiar fatherly tone that tore at my heart. "None of this is Abby's fault. It was me and Luke. We're the ones to take the blame. Point the gun my way." Papa motioned with his fingers, urging Doyle to swing his aim.

I stood transfixed, while the barrel of the gun pointed directly at me. Pure hatred darkened Doyle's eyes as he stared

The Chosen Child   *Joan Hall*

at me.

"Doyle, please listen," Edward tried to reason. "This has gone far enough." He stretched out a hand toward his brother.

For an instant, Doyle wavered. "I just wanted to be like Pa." He caught his breath on a half sob. "We had a right to defend our property. That stranger was a trespasser. Pa - Pa was a strong man and he wanted strong sons." Slowly he straightened his arm, deadening his aim at my chest. Doyle really hated me so much that he would pull the trigger.

"Dear God, please forgive my sins and accept my soul." I closed my eyes in preparation for the bullet to come.

"I warned you, Abby. I told you I would take you with me. If I'm to die then you die too."

"Doyle - no," Edward's shocked scream bounced off my eardrums.

"Don't make me shoot you, drop it," Sheriff Nolan yelled.

"Abby!" The plaintive cries of Chris and Papa rang in my ears, and I opened my eyes. In horror, I watched as Doyle cocked his weapon.

"Lord, help us," Preacher Allison called. The old man stood closest to me. Just as the explosion thundered through the air, the preacher threw himself in front of me. His body recoiled as the bullet struck, throwing him backward against

The Chosen Child   *Joan Hall*

me. A second explosion followed as Sheriff Nolan fired too. Doyle fell to his knees with his pistol hanging from his hand, a shocked expression marring his young face. For an instant, he remained on his knees then fell forward with his face in the dirt.

For stunned seconds, no one moved then Aunt Gertie dropped to the ground beside the preacher to cradle his head in her lap.

"The crazy fool," the sheriff stated as he stood over Doyle's form.

Edward threw himself over his brother, sobbing, "Doyle, Doyle." Over and over he cried out to rouse his brother from his unconscious state, but failed. Slowly, after his sobs subsided, he lifted his dazed face. He gripped Doyle's gun in his hand.

"Oh no," I gasped. Would this madness never end?

"Edward," the sheriff pleaded in short strained breaths, "Don't you think there's been enough killing? You're a good boy; I know you're a good boy. Don't get carried away with your grief."

Slowly Edward lifted the gun to point at his temple. He pleaded for understanding, his gaze encompassing us all. In a distorted, grieving voice, he cried, "I just can't go on alone. My brother and my Pa are both dead. We're all alike, so I'll just go and be with them. I tried to be good, like my Ma, but I sinned

The Chosen Child   *Joan Hall*

too, just as bad as Pa and Doyle." He sobbed, the great wrenching sounds of a breaking heart. "I didn't mean to do it, I swear before God himself, I didn't mean to kill Pa."

"Oh Edward," I moaned. My suspicion had been correct, but I had not wanted to hear the confession. It should have been Doyle.

"What happened, son?" Papa spoke softly, edging closer to Edward and Chris took hesitant steps in my direction.

"I just wanted to stop him, that's all. Pa didn't play fair. We all knew you never carried a gun," he said gazing into Papa's eyes. "We wrestled, but Pa was a lot stronger than me, so while he had me pinned down, I grabbed a rock and I hit him in the head. I thought he was just knocked out. I - I didn't even hit him hard. I took the pistol back to the house so it would be a fair fight between the two of you. I'm a killer too. I - I killed my own Pa. I don't deserve to live."

"What you did was well meant and I thank you for trying to help me," Papa said softly as he scooted closer to the distraught teen. "You probably saved my life. Why don't you put the gun down, you're only eighteen years old. You've got your whole life ahead of you."

"But I'll just spend it in jail. I'd die behind bars, so I just might as well go now." Edward squeezed his eyes tight together in preparation as he gripped the trigger.

"Wait," Sheriff Nolan called. "You won't have to go to jail; the death of your pa was an accident. As far as I'm concerned justice has been served. The way I see it, the two real culprits have already paid for their crimes. Does anybody see things any differently?" he asked as his gaze scanned us all. With nods of agreement, he turned to the agent. "What about it, Chris, will the government be charging Edward with a crime?"

"No, the government's case is closed," Chris said.

"There, see," the sheriff said. "You'll be free to live out the rest of your days. You can have a good life and make your Ma proud." Edward hesitated and a ray of hope lighted his face.

"You can raise a family," Papa added, "have lots of kids. Chloe would have liked having grandchildren, wouldn't she?"

"Yeah," the distressed youth said, a brief smile showing through his tears. "She loved babies."

"Put down that awful gun and let's close this case," the Sheriff prodded.

"Abby?" Edward made a last desperate plea to me. "Do you forgive me for the wrongs I done?"

Searching my heart, I recalled all the times he had come to my aid. "Of course I forgive you. You're a good person, Edward, and you deserve to live in peace."

"Do you forgive Doyle and Pa?" That was asking a lot of me. I glanced down at the preacher sprawled lifeless at my

The Chosen Child   *Joan Hall*

feet then lifted my gaze to the troubled youth who was legally my stepson. I had to forgive them, for if I couldn't, Edward would take his life in payment.

"Yes, yes, Edward, I forgive them." Chris was close enough to enfold me in his arms. Readily I collapsed against his strong chest.

"Come on, give me the gun," Papa urged, again stretching out his hand. Slowly Edward released the weapon, allowing it to fall. The sheriff rushed over and picked up the gun. With his other hand he felt for a pulse at Doyle's throat but sadly shook his head. "What about the preacher, Gert, is there any chance for him?"

Gazing down at the head she had been cradling in her lap, Aunt Gertie said in a stunned voice, "I don't know. I guess I just figured he was gone." Gingerly she felt around his throat. Her eyes brightened and her voice lifted to a youthful shrill. "He's alive. There's a good strong pulse here."

As if perfectly timed, the preacher stirred and moaned. My aunt touched the dark hole in his chest where the bullet had entered. "Praise the Lord," she cried. After tugging and pulling, she withdrew the Bible that Doyle had crammed beneath the preacher's shirt. The pages were torn and ragged where the bullet entered. Sticking her finger within the gaping space, she exclaimed, "The slug is still in here, it didn't enter him at all." After rubbing her hand over his chest, she declared, "Why, he ain't even hurt."

"What, what happened?" Preacher Allison stammered as consciousness returned.

"Oh, you brave, brave man," Aunt Gertie gushed as she rained kisses over the forehead and balding top of the old man's head. "You saved Abby, you saved our precious girl. With a little help from above," she conceded.

The gentleman rubbed the places where Gertie had planted her kisses of gratitude. A new awareness brightened his eyes. "Why Gertie, I didn't know you cared."

"Come on everybody," the sheriff said gruffly with the hint of a lump in his throat. "I think we just got a sign from above. This conflict has ended right here. Picking up the tattered Bible, he dug out the bullet with his finger then handed the book back to the preacher. "You might want to keep this as a reminder of His saving grace."

"I don't need a reminder," the preacher said matter-of-factly as he held the destroyed book.

Hesitantly, Edward stumbled over. He reached out and slowly took the book from the preacher's hand. "I'd like to keep this, if you don't mind," he said humbly. "That's one murder for which Doyle won't have to answer."

Together, we helped the old man to his feet. He and

The Chosen Child   *Joan Hall*

Aunt Gertie remained arm in arm as they began the hike back down the hill. Chris stayed close beside me with his arm about my waist. Sheriff Nolan and Papa walked side by side and following behind, alone, was Edward with his head downcast and the Bible clutched in his hand. Something compelled me to turn and gaze for a moment at the body slumped on the ground. The sight would linger in my memory forever as would the vision of poor William when I found him. Surely I would never have to witness such violence again, ever. I had seen enough for a lifetime.

A month had passed when I found myself sitting at my father's table pondering my future. Chris had returned to Washington to continue his work. He promised he would write soon but so far no letter had arrived.

Edward sold the farm and insisted that I take half of everything. With his share, he decided to start another life in Tennessee. Our parting had not been an emotional one. Too much lay between us for closeness now.

I had paid Papa the rest of the original IOU from Luke. The funds would buy Papa several head of cattle and make the farm more productive. He even talked of expanding the apple orchard. The hilltop flats did produce excellent fruit. Papa said he would market the apples as Potter's Best.

The Chosen Child   *Joan Hall*

Preacher Allison was calling on Aunt Gertie. She seemed happier than she had been since Uncle Walter died. Papa and the children seemed to be coping quite well in Mama's absence. So what was I to do now? My heart ached when I thought of Chris. Many times I relived the secretive stormy night of love lying with him in the barn loft and felt again the sweet ache his nearness brought.

"I swear child, are you mooning again?" Aunt Gertie floated across the kitchen amid a cloud of flour dust. "If that young man cares for you as much as I think he does, he'll be coming this way again soon."

"Do you really think so?" I asked her, hope evident in my voice.

"Yes, but he had better not wait too long. We're likely to have an early winter. I saw a wooly worm the other day and he was almost solid black."

"Oh, Aunt Gertie," I laughed. "It's just November and that worm was probably supposed to be black."

"Don't you go making fun of the signs. That is nature's way of preparing us for bad weather. You just have to be observant."

I could not argue with Aunt Gertie's wisdom. "I think I'll go for a walk," I said, anxious to be alone with my thoughts.

"Make sure you put on a sweater," my aunt called after

The Chosen Child   *Joan Hall*

me.

I decided to stroll down the lane. When Belle saw me she came loping over to tag behind. Edward had not objected when I asked to keep the hound. The dog took to her new home and the kids loved her. Lady, the mare, went to the new owner of the farm.

"Hi, Abby," Paul called from the barn, where he and the other children were romping in the hay. Silently I waved in return. The trees were just beginning to glow with the colors of fall. Bright yellows, oranges and reds scattered through the dark green foliage. A few colorful leaves fluttered down to rustle beneath my feet.

I reached down and patted Belle on the head. The animal wagged her tail and whined her pleasure. "I swear you are still the ugliest dog I have ever seen but I do love you. Come on," I said, urging the hound to walk with me.

Belle was first to notice the noise, stopping and piquing her ears in alarm. I spied the cause, a vehicle, turning from the main road into our lane. The car was silver grey in color and appeared shiny new. "I've never seen that car before," I said to my four-legged companion. "I wonder who would be coming to visit in a nice car like that."

The vehicle slowed when nearing where I stood and I glimpsed a blond head. Quickly, I smoothed my hair and

The Chosen Child   *Joan Hall*

tugged at the waistband of my skirt, making my appearance neater. My heart leapt and the sweetest sensation filled me, so wonderful, I almost ached with it. "Chris, Chris," I called in wonder. He had come back. Aunt Gertie was right.

Abruptly, the car stopped and my prince jumped out. He grabbed me and lifted me from the ground and swung me round and round. "Oh, I've missed you so." He sighed. "Oh, Abby, Abby." Finally he placed me back on the ground. Staring into my upturned face, he devoured me with his eyes. Slowly, he lowered his mouth and claimed mine in a kiss.

This is what love feels like, I thought as I melted against him. *This is where I belong, in Chris's arms.* For a long moment he clutched me against him then gently held me away at arms length so he could gaze into my eyes.

"Abby, I couldn't stay away. I know you're still young."

"I'm seventeen now," I interjected.

"And I know how much you love your family and your home here in Kentucky . . ."

"Yes," I conceded, "but I'm adventurous."

"But I'd like you to think about moving back to Virginia with me. I've been checking around. There's a very nice boarding school for young women close to where I live. I thought - I thought maybe you could enroll and we could see each other. I know you've been through a bad experience and

The Chosen Child   *Joan Hall*

our relationship is new but I - I think I'm in love with you and I hope you care about me too. And when you're older, I want to marry you. I . . . . I'll bring you back for visits . . . often."

"Yes, yes," I gushed. "I'll go with you." I couldn't believe my ears; my prince loved me as much as I loved him. "Let's go tell Aunt Gertie the news." I placed my arms around his neck.

Chris opened the car door for me to climb inside. Noticing Belle sitting on the ground, he pulled wide the back door and beckoned the animal in also. He said, "I swear that is the ugliest hound dog I have ever seen."

"Yes, but I love her."

"Then I love her too."

The End

The Chosen Child   *Joan Hall*